SECRET MAGIC

CHRONICLES OF THE MARKED BOOK TWO

S LAWRENCE

For information contact :

sglawrenceauthor@gmail.com

https://www.slawrencewriter.com/ sign up for my newsletter to stay up to date on new releases and for exclusive giveaways

Cover design by Sanja's Covers

ISBN: 978-1-950851-09-6

First Edition: 2021

❀ Created with Vellum

PROLOGUE

a week.

Not much time for a life to be completely changed. If I'm honest, it changed the moment I saw him floating in the water, near death.

A pirate.

They come on the tide, and death comes with them.

I didn't heed the warning. Everyone died. I watched my home burn as he dragged me away into the darkness of the night.

Swept out to sea and a new life. A life with five pirate captains and a destiny that both terrifies and calls to me.

It calls to me like the thing the Pirate King and many others search for.

The question is... Is it a siren luring me to my death or is it a power I was born to wield?

My captains believe the second; they believe I will save them all.

They offer the world with each of them by my side. It is tempting.

Someone watches, guiding and waiting for me to make

my decision. A god from the beginning of time, one that fought to save us in the war that almost destroyed the world.

If there is one, there might be more, and I have a feeling not all of them want me to succeed.

I look down at Liam, running my fingers over his velvety ears, and for the millionth time, question if I could be this woman they all think I am.

The King hunts for me, killing and worse to find me. The thought sends fear skating down my spine. I've seen the scars he left on my captains' backs; I heard the screams of those he killed in my village. I don't want to imagine what he would do to me.

If I'm the one destined to wield the power buried beneath the ice, I know he wouldn't kill me. I know my fate would be far worse.

It seems pain and heartache will happen no matter my choice.

Liam looks up and whines, and I follow his gaze. There they stand, waiting for me at the edge of the water—Fallon, Cyder, Hagen, Lash, and Wilder.

They don't seem to realize I've made my decision about them. They will be mine, and I will be theirs.

CHAPTER ONE
REYNA

"*O*pen it, Reyna." I'm so caught up in staring that I don't know which of them speaks but I reach out. My hand is shaking, my heart is pounding, and I'm gulping my breaths.

The top lifts easily, and my eyes widen.

The past can't be changed.

There, right on top, is a note written in beautiful masculine handwriting on fine paper. My hand shakes as I reach for it, stopping just before I touch it. It's not fear, not exactly; it's more like trepidation. Uncertainty that I'm worthy of this title that is being given to me.

I force my hand forward, closing my fingers on the paper gently and bringing it up close to my face. I get a whiff of some exotic scent and I wonder if it is from the person who wrote the words.

I've added this without the knowledge of the others. I will be watching, no matter the number of years. The others withdraw, feeling responsible for the destruction, but I will not. It has always been my purpose to help those on, let us call them, trips. You will be on a journey like nothing you can even dream. I saw the seer's face as she finished her entry and I have a feeling about what it might mean. So I will be near and help if I can.

Nestor, Guide and Protector ~ among other things.

Nestor. An unusual name. Guide. Protector. More? Could he be one of those that had fought in the war? Or did he watch as others unleashed their power on the world.

"What does it say?" Wilder is watching me closely, even as Cyder leans in trying to see.

I hand the note to Wilder and say, "It is from a person named Nestor."

Fallon looks down into the box. "There's more inside."

I look down and see multiple notes folded inside the box. Overwhelmed—that's the feeling that washes through me. My chest becomes tight as I struggle to breathe.

"I'm taking her to my ship." Cyder's voice is close to my ear, and I feel muscled arms come around me, lifting me. "Bring the chest. She can look at it when she is ready."

His tone is that of a captain, and none of the others argue. I don't fight the hand that holds my head against his chest. I feel his strength as he carries me across the deck and even more strength as he swings us across to the next ship. I can hear at least one of the others following behind us. Cyder's boots hit the deck of his ship and he carries me to the Captain's quarters. I don't look up until he places me on a chair. Blinking, I look around and take in his domain.

It is wholly Cyder. Gorgeous shades of greens and golds. The chair I'm sitting on is overstuffed, the fabric faded but still beautiful, plaid with gold edging, the threads bare, but it practically hugs me.

The whole room is reminiscent of a cool forest. I can picture him standing among the trees, the scent of wood and earth wrapping around us. He stands silent, waiting for my judgement.

"Thank you," I murmur, looking up at him.

"There is no hurry, no need to rush. This thing has been hidden for hundreds of years, so you don't need to rush blindly to it today." He sounds so sure, and I can't help but feel calmer. "You can hide here for as long as you want."

"I don't want to hide," I start to argue, but he shakes his head.

"Maybe that was the wrong word. I meant take your time. Read through the notes, digest the information. You might be this chosen one, but that doesn't mean you have no say in how any of this works."

I stare up at the most quiet of the five, the one who has watched me since the moment he saw me on the rocks with Fallon. Cyder is the one who pushed, who was unconvinced I was some mythical creature sent to save the world. The one who is maybe even still unconvinced.

"Do you believe I'm the person everyone thinks I am?" I ask, not in judgement but more wishing he would convince me.

"I didn't." He kneels in front of me, staring into my eyes. "But maybe I do now. If all of this is real, why can't you be the one to lead us from this darkness? Why can't we be the ones to help you?"

"I might not be strong enough."

He takes my hands in his, and I like the roughness of them, like he pulls the ropes that raise his sails.

"That's why you have us." He squeezes. "We are your strength when you don't have enough."

I feel something shift in me, something settles. He hasn't really spoken to me before, and I like the sound of his voice and the golden ring around the hazel of his eyes. He reminds me of the dragons I've seen in my books hidden in the woods.

I look and see he had closed the door behind us. We have

5

never been alone. His eyes look back over his shoulder, then he turns them back to me.

"Do you want me to leave?" He studies my face, his eyes watching for my reaction, watching for any hint of rejection.

He finds none.

"I want to know you."

He is the quiet one, not like Hagen, who is watching and learning. Quiet as in he doesn't see the need for many words. I relish that he has spent so many on me. It makes me feel special in a way I can't explain.

"I am an open book."

I want to laugh but smirk instead. An open book, he is not. "Do you like books?"

"Not much use for them, but there are a few that I've enjoyed." His head tilts slightly, a bemused look on his face.

"What did you like about them?"

"The pictures." He returns my smirk as I roll my eyes.

"Can I see?"

His eyes shutter for a moment, guarding what he holds dear. I understand not wanting to get hurt. He understands it's a test. He gets up and walks over to a shelf built into the wall of the ship. I hear a low growl and smile. Someone has brought Liam to me. Fallon must have. I stand and cross to the door, opening it. He bounds in, passing me by, only stopping when he is near Cyder. I watch as he sits near the chair I had just been in, his head turned toward the man at the bookshelf.

Liam has never steered me wrong when it comes to people. He wouldn't have accepted these men if they weren't good. But I can tell he has questions when it comes to Cyder, just like I do. Not questions about what kind of man he is, just more about how much he wants from me.

I think about Fallon's words, of how we must learn to trust each other, but how do we do that when we don't know each other? These questions, the answers are how it happens, but I'd be a fool to think it will happen quickly. I know we will move forward and then have moments of uncertainty for a very long time. Maybe forever.

Generations of distrust are bred into my blood, and they have been demonized their entire life by people just like me.

That thought stops me, makes every part of my body freeze for a heartbeat.

When I blink, he is in front of me, a worn book clutched in his hands and a look of curiosity in his eyes.

"Where were you?" His voice is low and rumbles through me, shaking the thoughts and loosening my muscles.

"Just thinking of how we could change the world."

He frowns, confused. "Isn't that the point, you changing the world?"

"Not me...we," I whisper as I reach my hand out and cover his on his book.

I can tell he doesn't understand and honestly, I don't know how to explain it completely. I just know that at the end of this, the world will be a better place.

"Show me your book."

He doesn't move for a moment, but slowly under my hand, I can feel his fingers loosening. My heart beats slowly as I stare up into his eyes. He turns the book and places it in my hand.

"Wilder found it in a museum when we found the ships." He smiles but it looks more like a grimace as he glances down at the book. "He gave it to me after we all picked places we thought we might have come from."

"You chose this place?" I look down at the cover and its beautiful golden designs.

"I chose these people—the Celts, Druids, the Irish and Scottish. I saw myself in images of them. When I read stories of them, I felt them in my soul." His vehemence raises the hairs on my arms and neck.

I picture a story I had read of a highland warrior, some story of love, and I can imagine him in the role. I notice for the first time the tiny thin braids that start at his temples and are pulled back in the longer hair he has tied back. I hadn't paid attention to my Celtic warrior, for he had quietly stood in the background as the others circled me. Watching. Waiting for his moment. Like a warrior from the old times, he took his moment when he knew it was right, swooping me up and away. Saving me from myself.

Liam bumps into me and I glance down. He is pushing his head against the man in front of me. Claiming him. It makes me smile. How appropriate of my gentle giant of a wolfhound, picking the warrior for his own.

Cyder looks down then drops to his knees, his hands cupping Liam's big head and fingers scratching at his floppy ears. He leans close and whispers low in one of those ears and then moves back slightly to look into another set of eyes ringed in gold.

Liam woofs and then licks up his cheek, and a giggle breaks from my throat. "He likes you."

"He respects me. I don't think this beast likes anyone but you." Cyder gives him one last scratch before he pushes up in front of me once more.

I don't disagree but I know Liam, and he has chosen. He might trust the others to keep me safe and he might love me the most but he is choosing to let this man into his life. It makes my chest tighten, and a rush of jealousy hits me. I feel shame in the next moment. Liam needs a family just as I do.

I look down at my protector and smile when he turns his eyes up to mine. I see understanding; I see hope for us both and I grab it with both hands.

I step forward, pressing my body against Cyder's, and

raise up, kissing him gently. He remains stiff but kisses me back softly, surprising me. Slowly, his hands come around me, and I feel him relax a little.

His kiss changes, becomes deeper, and the taste of him hits me like a shot of the alcohol my dad had hidden behind barrels at the pub. He had found it hidden deep in the forest in the ruin of an old home. Dark amber and smoky, it had conjured thoughts of far away lands and music I had never heard. It is fitting for my captain.

He breaks away, leaving me wanting to sip more, and I lick over my lower lip. A noise breaks from him, half growl and half moan, and my body clenches. Once again, I'm surprised by my desire for each of them.

Did the old gods have a hand in this need that is building in me?

I don't know if I should be angry or thankful at the thought of them meddling with us all.

"Does it bother you?" I murmur, still clutching at his shirt even though I don't remember grabbing the fabric with my hand.

The book is still in my other hand but it's now pressed into his chest.

"What?" His breath is warm on my face.

"That we may have no say in any of this. That someone might have designed all of this." I move my hand between us.

"I'd be a liar if I said I was okay with anyone being in control of me. So, yes, it bothers me, but I have to believe if you are destined for greatness, destined to save the entire world, they have to mean you well. They have to want you to be happy. I love my brothers and I would do anything to make sure they find peace. You could be the keeper of their peace."

He looks surprised by the amount of words that have left his mouth, and I grin before letting it fade away.

"What about your peace?"

"I don't know if there is peace for me." He's honest, and it hurts my heart for him.

"We could try," I offer, and it's slightly selfish since I'm hoping to find my own peace with them.

Dark dreams have been plaguing my sleep, dreams filled with screams, my own and others. I always wake to sweat coating my body and images of me beneath a pirate racing through my head. I haven't told them about the dreams but I know Wilder and Fallon have watched me as I struggle to calm my mind and body.

Violence like what happened that night had never come to my home before then, so I had never understood the fear people had whispered about until the night was filled with it. I know even now that I don't truly understand it because I was not taken. I was saved, protected by Fallon, by one of my captains.

"You're thinking again." His smile is barely a curve, and I realize other than his outburst of laughter I had heard the first day, I haven't seen him smile or joke.

"I was thinking, how can I be outraged over not having a say when they sent you all to me? Fallon saved me. Hagen saved me. You are saving me. Wilder and Lash are saving me. They knew what I would need and sent me five men that could provide it all. It seems selfish and childish to complain about it. I know that we will struggle to find our way but I have to be grateful that I wasn't taken, or worse, that night."

It seems like a lifetime ago and yet fresh, but fading with each encounter with those protecting me, helping me, and loving me.

"I don't know if we saved you or you saved us but I'm glad that Fallon washed up on your rocks." He smiles slightly once more. We both hear footsteps near the door, and he steps back from me. "Read some of the stories, relax for a bit, and then if you want, I will help you look through the chest, or we can wait for the others." He moves to go around me but pauses long enough to bend slightly and kiss me on the cheek quickly before walking quickly to the door. He can't see the huge smile on my face.

A warrior with a sweet side.

Sighing, I move to the chair and sit, tucking the book at my side as I lean over Liam's head. "We are going to be okay here, aren't we?" He nuzzles into my neck, and I feel the last of my apprehension leaving me. "You want to learn about the Celts?"

I had often spent hours reading out loud to my friend in the forest. He woofs gently as he settles down, laying over my foot and leaning against my leg. I throw my other leg over the arm of the chair, breaking my mother's rule, and I can't help but feel her here with me.

Opening the book, I begin to read of a land that sounds magical and make-believe, but it also calls to me, sings to my soul, and I understand what my fierce warrior had spoken of.

CHAPTER TWO
CYDER

*S*he is a goddess, like those the Druids worshipped.

I am willing to sacrifice myself to her. I will sacrifice the King to her, if she asks.

Forcing myself away from the door, I head over to my first mate. He is waiting, watching me too closely.

"Mind ye business, Travis," I snap and he just grins, unfazed by my mood.

He's been with me since almost the very beginning and is used to my shortness.

"Ye keeping the girl, Captain?" He seems entirely too interested for my comfort.

"If I am, she is no concern of yours." I stake my claim and make it clear to him that she is off limits. I know Travis will spread the word.

"Didn't think she was, Captain."

I don't fall for his sweet tone but I know he wouldn't cross any line set for him.

"She is important to you so she's important to us. Nothing more, nothing less. Kellihan has spread the word that we are to consider her ours." His tone of reverence surprises me.

I'm only surprised by the reverence, not the fact that Kellihan had spread the word. Fallon's cook was the unspoken leader of all the crews, and his word is law. Memories flash through my mind of him caring for us before we were tossed into the sea to die. The old man is the closest thing we had to family or a father after we were ripped from our mother's arms. The image of my mother's face flashes; the last time I saw her, it was twisted in fear and pain. Shaking my head, I try to thrust it away to where I keep it locked. It helps me to see her as I try to remember her. It is mostly just flashes of her smile. I no longer remember her voice or the feel of her arms, only her smile. I swallow hard, fighting the feelings threatening to overwhelm me.

"You okay, Captain?"

I blink at Travis's words, suddenly reminded I'm not alone. "Fine. Reyna will be staying as we sail through the canal. Have the cook bring up food. Tell him to make it good, for the other ships' cooks have been wowing her with their food."

"I will make sure he thinks our pride is on the line." Travis smirks. "The others are already unfurling their sails; are you ready to get under sail also?"

I look to the other ships, just beginning to move away from us. "Let them get a short distance away but keep them in sight," I murmur as I glance at my quarters.

"Understood." Travis turns sharply on his heel and starts toward the stairs, but I don't miss the chuckle he tries to cover with his hand.

He is not wrong in his assumptions; I do want her to myself, unable to flee to another ship. I've seen the way she looks at the others. I see how she feels for them already, but there is no look like that in her eyes as she looks at me. Interest maybe, but no feelings. Not yet.

I've always liked a challenge.

The biggest challenge in this case will be me. I understand it, but even the knowledge won't make it any easier for me to change my behavior or be less caustic to her. I don't know how to be sweet like Wilder. I can't be the strong silent type like Hagen. Fallon is the best of us, so it's no surprise that she has fallen for him.

I am not soft or lovable. Staring out at the glassy water, I wonder how I might win a small part of her heart.

The thought gives me pause. I have wanted her since she stepped upon my deck with the beast at her side, but when did that desire change to more? Was it the tender looks she bestows on my brothers or when she dove into the water to save Hagen? Maybe when she climbed into my lap, teasing both Lash and myself.

Glancing back at my door, I wonder how to be a companion to her. Lover, I know, but more than that is foreign to me. I rarely spend time with a woman, and when I do, it's in the bed, not out of it. How does a man woo a woman?

Jewels, dresses, or win her in bed so she must love you out of it? I can do all of those. I stalk across the deck and head down the stairs. I stride through the ship to the kitchen.

"Oliver?" I get the man's attention.

"Aye, Captain?" He turns his head but continues to stir whatever he is cooking in the pot.

"Dinner? You know Kellihan pulled out the stops, wooed her with coconut." I sniff the air, trying to get an idea of what he might be cooking. Spices filled the small kitchen.

He looks offended. "I can out cook that old man any day, and ye know it. I'm bringing the Latin flair." He lifts the spoon and holds it out to me, his hand cupped underneath it. "I used some of the meat the beast brought down."

I blow it once before drawing the steaming food into my mouth. The chunks of meat are spicy but not too hot, and the cubed potatoes are perfectly cooked, neither hard or mushy. It is delicious. An explosion of flavor.

"You've outdone yourself, Oliver."

"Thank you for always getting me the spices, sir." His chest has swelled at my compliment.

"I had confidence in you." I pat him on his shoulder as he turns back to the pot.

"I'm also making bread and a dessert, Captain." He preens.

"I'm looking forward to it," I say as I turn to leave the galley.

I make my way through the rest of the ship, heading to my hidey hole and my treasure. Moving barrels around, I make my way through the maze to the very front of my ship. There, tucked against the sternpost, flush against the keelson, is my chest. My brothers keep theirs in their quarters, but I hide mine away. Trust doesn't come easily to any of us, but I like my crew and would hate if any of them did something stupid.

Temptation can get the better of any man, myself included.

I've caught myself glancing at my brother's hiding spots more than once. I run my hands over the carved top, where I had copied some of the designs in the book I had given to Reyna. The edges of the designs are worn smooth from my fingers rubbing over them. Hell, maybe I moved the chest here to keep myself from obsessing over it and the items it holds. I can understand why Reyna's eyes keep returning to the chest she brought with her. It too is covered in beautiful carvings, different from those on mine but similar.

It could mean something, but I doubt it. I shake my head

at my own foolishness. I can't believe I'm getting caught up in Wilder's fantasies. I agreed to keep her with us because I'm tired of being alone and I want my brothers happy, not because I believe in destiny and magic. Although, her power over the sea creatures does seem otherworldly.

Magic.

If I believe that, I have to believe the rest and I'm not sure I'm ready for that. Instead of facing either possibility, I look down at my chest once again. Pushing the secret pin hidden on the back, I unlock the box and lift the lid. It opens easily and reveals its contents.

Wilder had focused on books when we found the city, and the others had each found things that drew them, things they thought would be useful to us. I had focused on finding things like I had seen on the King's ship, the things that I had been whipped for seeing. He had a trove of jewels and gold and he didn't like for anyone to know of it.

My skin on my back crawls, the scars tightening as the memories cascade through my mind. I can feel the whip cutting my flesh, and my fingers tighten on the chest as my breath comes in gulps. Sweat drips off my nose, the drops darkening the fabric that covers my most prized possession .

It has been a very long time since the memories have taken hold of me like this. Reyna is stirring up things I can't control. I hate being out of control, for it reminds me too much of before we were thrown from the King's ship.

My grandmother's face floats in front of my eyes. It is an exact replication of the last moment I saw her, hands outstretched, grasping at my sweater as I was ripped from her. I had screamed for her until I watched him kill her, his eyes focused on my own. It was the first of many acts meant to break me.

Shaking my head, I force the other memories threatening my sanity away, back down to the bottom of the deep, where

I keep them locked for everyone's safety. Each of us have demons; I just can't let mine out. Unlike Lash's, who is happy between a woman's legs, or Hagen's, who is calmed by weapons, mine wants only to destroy.

I destroy everything and everyone around me. I revel in the chaos I create and the pain I cause until I gain control, and then the regret crushes me. Travis and the rest of the crew recognize the signs of both phases. Unfortunately, they have had to deal with the fallout from more than one episode.

This time, instead of blindly letting go of my control, I try to focus on why I came to my chest, to my treasure. Reyna.

I look down at the priceless items, my hoard. My fingers touch a ruby before moving to a diamond necklace. I had found these things throughout the city. Shops had stood forgotten, dust inches thick over cases filled with treasures. I had loaded carts full of things long forgotten and rarely seen since the battle. Some things are on my brother's ships—chandeliers, paintings, statues—beautiful things that deserved to be brought into the world once more.

Things that deserved to be loved. Things like Reyna.

Where are these thoughts coming from? Love? Cherished?

Has she changed us so much already?

"Obviously," I mumble as I focus on my treasure once more. "Why else are you here looking for something to win her over?"

I'm right and I'm talking to myself. I shake my head as I try to find something perfect. What would be perfect? I don't know her well. I don't know what I'm even looking for.

My fingers stray to the emerald green cloth and I smile. I had been surprised when I found it in the shop so long ago. It had been out of place among the jewels. It had been old, very old, ancient even, and it had called to me, resonated like a crystal bell inside me.

Unfolding the fabric, I look at the pendant and the delicate looking chain it hangs on.

Unlike the other things in the store made of gold or silver and encrusted with jewels of every color, this necklace was simple. The bronze was worn and tarnished, and even the chain was old, made from loops of the same bronze. It should be easily bent and broken but it's strong.

Rocking back on my heels, I find myself shaking my head once again. Just like Reyna is strong. Damn Wilder and his stories of destiny and magic. I run my fingers through my hair, my eyes locked on the necklace. Maybe I should start with something less important, less symbolic.

Shifting, I look at my other container, the one that contains paintings. I think of the ones I had taken from the museum, but none of those seem quite right. Then I think of the small gallery that stood between two antique shops. The artists had been locals, the images painted of the city and area around it and its people. I had taken many of them, but one is vibrant in my mind. The woman was breathtaking, and the artist had captured her lost in thought. Even I could tell he had loved her.

I pull at the side of the crate, opening the panel, and move the canvases around until I find it. Sliding it free of the crate, I hold it out at arm's length. Bright colored hair frames big eyes, and she is caught in a shaft of light as she sits beneath the branches of an old oak tree, moss hanging down to wrap her in an air of mystery. A man watches her from beneath another tree. I don't know if I had noticed him before, but now my eyes keep focusing on him.

"Because you have been doing the same damn thing, you fool." I have been watching Reyna, letting her look at my brothers with so much feeling in her wide eyes. "Time to join her or walk away."

The painting is perfect. An offering for more. A promise of more.

Setting it to the side, I push the panel back into place, then move the other things back in front of the crate. I wrap the necklace back in the green fabric before closing the lid of the chest, listening for the click of the lock. It only takes me a few moments to put the wooden crates back around my treasure trove. Standing, I pick the painting up and then as I move through the maze, I shift different crates back into place, hiding the way to my stash.

I can smell dinner as I make my way down the narrow hallway. I pause outside the galley once more, saying nothing.

"I'll be right behind you, sir."

I nod. "Take your time."

Stepping away, I continue through the belly of the ship, passing members of the crew, nodding at some, ignoring the looks of interest from others.

I climb up into the afternoon sun, stunned that the light makes the painting and the woman in it even more beautiful. Crystals glisten like diamonds, replicating stars in the woman's eyes. Others tinted slightly green twinkle within the tree's dropping branches. I can see golden ones shimmer in the night sky. Fireflies. Lifting the painting close to my face, I try to make out what the artist had used but there isn't a piece big enough to identify them.

The person was a true artist, the strokes delicate but bold. My collection of books consists of legends and art. People who create fascinate me.

I stood staring at the painting long enough for the sun to sink lower in the sky. A noise forces me to turn, and there she stands with the door to my cabin open, her eyes locked on the painting in my hands.

"It's beautiful." Her voice is breathy and filled with emotion.

"It's for you." I hold it out as I turn to her. "A gift."

"For me?" She steps away from the door, and now those brilliant eyes are locked on my face.

"Yes. I thought..." I pause, unsure of how to say what I'm thinking. "I thought you might want to hang it, to make my home your home." I don't say 'to choose me, to love me.'

She smiles shyly, moving closer, and I let her take the canvas from my hands.

"I love it." She lets her eyes travel around the woman's face, almost caressing it. "She is magnificent."

"Shall we see where to hang her?" I ask, holding out my hand and hoping she takes it.

She nods as she transfers the painting to one hand then places her smooth palm into mine. My fingers close around hers slowly, and she tightens hers around mine, starting forward and pulling me along behind her. The beast is lying across my couch and doesn't even pretend that he might get down. She stops near the table, releasing my hand and spinning around to look for a spot for the woman.

"She needs to be in the light but not directly, so she doesn't fade." My voice is low but it draws her eyes to me once again.

She nods and looks around once more. I have my bed across from the window so I can wake to the morning light. She chews at her lip.

"What are you thinking? Ask," I urge her, wanting to hear her wants.

"I was thinking it would be beautiful to wake up and see the sun on it."

I blink, imagining it—her naked body against mine as the

morning light glimmers over the painting, lighting it from within. Her body would be glowing just like the painting in that morning sun.

"I'm sorry if I overstepped." She looks away.

"No. Let's move the bed. It would be beautiful." I don't add the thoughts I had about her being beautiful in the same light.

"Really?" Her happiness will be worth the work this will take.

I nod as I turn to call for help. She doesn't need to move the hulking bed frame. When I turn back, she is standing on the mattress and holding the painting up at the wall. She glances at me, and the smile on her face makes my heart stutter.

Footsteps force me to shove the emotions roiling just beneath the surface down.

"Captain?" One of the younger, newer boys stands in the open door, waiting for instruction.

"I need you to help me move the bed to the opposite wall."

Reyna jumps down, moving aside as he moves quickly to the other side across from me. I move to the edge of the bed and bend down, grasping the carved wood. I had found the bedframe in the city and forced the others to help me get it to the ship.

I had often wondered how our ships had gotten to the city. They were unlike any others we found there. Five ships from days long gone moored all along the river's bank. At first, I thought, like the others, that they had been sailed there right after the battle, the city found by survivors. But long ago, I realized if that had been true, surely there would have been people living in the city. But there was no one. It was a ghost town. It was as if all of the destruction of the war had been wiped away.

Hagen had found a small globe of glass with a city inside

it, and snow fell when you shook it. That was what New Orleans had been like, a city under a globe.

We set the bed down, having shifted it across the room. I had liked the bed because the headboard and the footboard were the same, with delicately carved designs in hardwood, wood polished and oiled until it is almost black.

Once we get it set into place, the boy leaves the room silently. Her fingers run over the carvings, like they had the door to Fallon's quarters. I cannot boast doing these myself; I don't have the talent he does. But the sight of her fingers caressing over the wood causes my stomach to tighten. Need crawls through me. Her fingers fall away as she moves back to the wall, and I watch as I try to control my desires.

Thunder claps loudly. I glance out the window, seeing clouds rolling toward us. She looks back at me and then out at the clouds.

"Can you hold it?"

I nod and join her in front of the wall, taking the painting from her. She spins away, throwing herself onto the covers. Laying back, she curls on her side, tucking her hand beneath my pillow. Her eyes are fixed on mine, and I don't try to hide my desires this time.

A knowing smile curves her full lips. "Can you move it slightly up and to the right?"

I do as she asks without taking my eyes off her.

"Perfect."

"I agree." I let my need creep into my voice, her cheeks flush the prettiest shade of peachy-pink.

I mark the spot, then set the painting down. I've already grabbed a nail from a cup I keep on a small shelf. I reach for a smooth round stone on the table that had been beside the head of the bed. I use it like a hammer, striking the nail three times before placing it back where it had been.

The painting has a thin wire on the back that I had seen

before. Bending, I pick it up and turn to look at her with it in my hands. She has pushed up, leaning on her elbows as she watches me.

I'm just about to turn when I see her brows draw down. "What's wrong?"

"What does that say?" She pushes up farther, coming to her knees as she moves toward me on the bed.

I hold it out to her instead of turning it so I can see it.

"Oh, my God." Her hand is shaking as she reaches out for the painting.

Now I can't help but angle it so I can see what she sees.

"Cora." I read the name out loud, but it means nothing to me. "By Remy Sinclair." The signature is full of flourish, barely legible. "Do you know the name?"

"It's who wrote the journal and the letter. Remy. He wrote about Cora." She touches the woman's face, feather light. "She is beautiful. He loved her. Can you see it?"

"Yes. I thought so when I was looking at it below when I picked it." I say the words, but my mind is racing.

What are the chances of me finding a painting by the man at the center of all of this?

Destiny. Magic. Prophecy.

Looking back at her face, I can see the same thoughts are blowing through her mind.

Thunder claps again, this time vibrating the ship just as a flash of lighting causes the painting to shimmer. The sky has turned dark, and rain begins to beat against the glass of the window.

I hang the painting as I feel the ship slow, the sails have been drawn. Turning back to her, I see her raised up, hands gripping the wood, her eyes glazed with emotion. I step to her, my hands coming up to frame her face. I lower my head slowly, savoring the slight flare of her pupils.

She closes the distance, her lips pressing against mine as

her hands grip at my shirt to pull me closer. I fight the desire to throw her back, to rip the clothes from her body.

'How had my brothers done this?'

It's my last coherent thought before I lose myself in the taste of her, in the feel of her tongue. The taste of it is like the strongest liquor. She goes straight to my head. I draw her deeper into my mouth wanting to devour her.

A knock startles and irritates me. "WHAT?" I growl as I tear away from her heat.

Her breath is coming in shallow gasps, and her eyes say she is just as irritated by the interruption.

"Dinner, Sir."

"Enter." I say it even when I want to send him away but I had agreed with my brothers to take our time, to win her heart along with her body.

"Saved by the knock." She giggles while straightening her shirt.

"I'm sorry, I didn't realize..." I hadn't even known I had touched her clothes.

"You should probably fix your own." She grins while letting her eyes drift down.

I glance down and see my shirt is pulled loose and wide open. I wasn't the only one who had been lost in the moment. I don't bother straightening mine, letting it mark her mine. Oliver will spread the word, for the man can't keep a secret to save his life.

The door opens and he leads a group of men inside. Each carries a tray with glorious smelling food. The table is covered when they are finally finished. I pull out the chair for Reyna.

"I hope you enjoy it, Miss." Oliver beams.

"I'm sure I will. It smells amazing. Like nothing I've ever had."

She smiles at him, and I watch as she captures another

heart without even trying. I don't listen as he explains each dish but I do watch as she tastes each. The sounds of pleasure and look of ecstasy on her face is enough to make me want to throw him overboard.

"Oliver, that will be all," I grit out adding, "Thank you." After seeing her face.

"Cyder." She frowns at me.

"Yes, of course, Sir. Enjoy, Miss." Oliver leaves before she can stop him.

"That was rude, Cyder," she admonishes me as soon as the door closes.

Admonishes. Me. On my own ship.

"I am Captain here." It comes out hard, harder than I meant.

"I know that but…" She stops, her fork moving as her fingers relax and tighten over and over. "I'm sorry, I don't have the right."

Fuck. I've ruined it already.

"That wasn't exactly what I meant." How do I say I want to share no part of her with others when I've agreed to do just that with my brothers? "I just meant the crew needs to remember their place."

The look on her face says that's not a bit better in her mind.

Silence is thick for long minutes as she pushes food around her plate. I've ruined the whole meal for her.

"I'm…"

"How…"

We both start at the same time, and she smiles sadly, motioning for me to continue.

"You first, Reyna." I steel myself for her words.

"How do you see this working between us all?"

Shit. Straight to the point, straight to the heart of it.

"I…we agreed to… share sounds just fucking shitty but I

can't think of another way to say it. I'm not articulate like Wilder and Fallon." I wipe over my face, knowing I am driving her away from me.

Something inside me clenches. My heart, maybe.

"I had hoped we would be a family." She reaches a hand out across the table, and I just look at it for a moment before covering it with my own. "To do that, we have to trust each other."

"I trust my brothers with my very life." The words are a declaration.

"And me?" Her words are no more than a whisper.

I don't respond. Do I trust her? How can I?

"I don't know you yet. I want you, have since you stepped on my ship with that beast." I jerk my head at Liam, still sleeping on the couch.

She smiles, and I'm even more confused than I have been since she arrived.

"If you had said you trusted me, I wouldn't have believed you. I want to earn your trust. I don't know how I will but I hope you give me a chance. Fallon told me women haven't been allowed on your ships." I nod. "So it must be just as confusing for your crewmen."

She grows quiet, and I feel like a heel. "I will talk to Oliver. Apologize." I draw a breath and grip her hand a bit harder. "I must also apologize to you. I can only say I am unused to the emotions I feel when I'm around you."

"I feel the same way, Cyder." She leans on her elbow, looking at me intently, an emotion I'm not sure of in her eyes. "I haven't felt anything like this before."

"Like what, exactly?" I let my voice drop, let my hunger fill my eyes as my gaze travels down her neck and along the opening of her shirt.

"Wanting so much." She doesn't elaborate.

Part of me wants to hear it, but I won't force her. I know from Fallon she is innocent.

"I was with a boy from my village, but it was nothing like this."

She glances away from me, which is good because I can't hide my shock.

"Did you think I was a virgin?" She smirks at me.

"I...no...I just...we..." I sputter out, not wanting to offend her.

She doesn't say anything, and as the seconds crawl by, I begin to worry I've completely blown it, but just a moment later, she starts to laugh. Her hand pats at my hand. Relief rushes through me, but she sobers quickly.

"Does it make a difference?" She studies me, watching for my reaction. "That I'm not?"

"No." I feel an anger rising in me, anger that she would be worried that we would shun her for having been with a man before she even knew us. "We all have pasts, and you shouldn't feel bad or worry about having found satisfaction with someone you had feelings for."

She visibly relaxes.

"I've seen it happen in my home," she utters softly, bringing her glass to her lips and sipping.

"There are no double standards on our ships." I'm firm, promising.

"Have you shared a woman before?" Her words are filled with curiosity and possibly a hint of jealousy.

"No. Well, maybe Lash and Hagen but not the rest, as far as I know." I don't miss the hint of heat that flares in her eyes.

Interesting. It opens a whole new train of thought in my mind.

"I'm still working out how this will all work."

"I think we all are." I watch as she takes a bite, savoring the flavors.

"This is so good," she mumbles, getting another bite ready while she still chews.

I reach over and uncover the dessert. Travis has made a sweet cream dessert with a caramel sauce drizzled over it. He has only made something like this once before, back when he was trying to get the job as cook on the ship.

She chews slower as she looks at the dessert. Finally she swallows the food in her mouth and lets the fork slowly lower back to the plate, the next bite on it forgotten. I pull her plate out of the way and push the dessert in front of her. She looks up at me and licks over her bottom lip.

I hold out a spoon, and she reaches for it, letting her fingers slide over mine. I might have made a mistake in this. I know this from the gleam in her eyes. She dips the spoon into the cream, then lifts it toward her mouth. The tip of her tongue flicks out, tasting the sweetness before curling back in between her lips.

I watch, picturing that tongue curling around parts of me. My brothers and I had agreed to go very slow. I don't want to wait. She holds out a spoon of cream, and I lean forward, drawing the sweetness into my mouth. I can see I'm not the only one affected by her game. Pushing back, I stand and move around. Drawing her up, I push the dishes from the side of the table and lift her up. Her eyes widen but then darken with desire.

I take the spoon from her hand and scoop some of the delicate dessert. Her mouth opens slightly in anticipation, but instead of taking it to her luscious lips, I let it dribble into the cleft between her breasts.

She leans back, giving me instant access. Vixen. Temptress. Sea Witch. She is everything. She is awakening things in each of us. I'm ravenous for her, not just her body but for all of her.

"I must taste you," I growl at her neck.

"I think you will be tasting sugar." She laughs, but it is breathless.

"It will keep me from becoming addicted to you. We all said slow," I murmur against her collarbone.

"I think I will grow tired of this slow," she responds as her hand skates into my hair, pushing my head farther down.

I wonder if she can feel my feral smile against her flushed skin. I lick the cream off that heated flesh tasting the essence of her beneath the sweetness.

CHAPTER THREE
REYNA

I can sense the wildness in him and I want to get lost in it.

Letting my mind drift away, the worries of how a relationship with these men will work fade for the moment. Instead, I focus on the subtle scratching of his short beard rubbing over my sensitive flesh.

Lightning flashes beyond my eyelids that have fallen closed, and the clap of thunder that follows it vibrates the wooden table beneath me. The ship shifts sharply and I grasp at Cyder as his head comes up.

His jade gaze looks to the skies outside and a frown creases his brow. I hide the smile that threatens to break across my face. He has cream in the hairs around his mouth.

Reaching up, I run my thumb over his lips catching the sweetness on the pad before moving it to my own lips. His eyes lock onto it as I draw it inside my mouth.

"The storm is about to rage." He sounds a bit strangled. "I should go and help the crew."

He says it but makes no effort to move away from me.

"Is it bad being in a storm while on the seas?" I feel apprehension at the thought of being tossed around helplessly in the winds.

"It can be exciting," he murmurs, still looking at my lips.

I reach my hands out to clasp his face and bring him to me, kissing him soundly and quickly. "Go if you must. I will stay here, waiting."

He nods before turning away and walking briskly to the door. He pauses there before pulling it open. Liam stretches and slides off the couch, following in Cyder's steps.

"Can you let him out? I still need to figure out how to deal with his needs." I feel embarrassed.

"The crew has set up an area with grass. One of them had thought of it when we were close to shore. It is small but it should be enough for your friend's needs."

My mouth falls open at their thoughtfulness. "I don't know what to say. That they would even think of Liam, of me..." I fall silent, looking beyond him to the movement of his men on the deck.

"They already love their queen." He bows his head and steps out, waiting for Liam to pass him before closing the door.

I'm still sitting on the table when a knock at the door startles me. Jumping down, I straighten my clothes, making sure that there are no remnants of the dessert on my skin.

"Come in," I call out moments later.

Oliver pokes his head in. "I came to clear things away before the waves get too bad, miss."

"Of course, Oliver. Could you leave the dessert? I would like to eat more of it." I wave my hand at the rest. "Everything was amazing. You truly are an accomplished chef."

He looks sheepish but pleased as he moves the plates and dishes to the tray he had brought them on.

"Will the night be bad?" I ask as he rushes to finish.

"It could be, miss, but we will keep you safe. The Dragon is a sound vessel, my queen."

"Oh, no, I'm not a queen and certainly not yours." I feel flustered at his words.

"One queen to rule them all," Oliver murmurs as he picks up the tray and hurries to the door. "We all know who you be, miss." He dips his head as he backs out the door.

"Indeed." They might know, but I don't have a clue.

The ship rolls as rain starts to hit the glass of the window. My heart pounds and I grab the edge of the table trying to steady myself. My stomach roils with my emotions.

I hear loud barking and the sound of claws on the door and I leap up to open the door to let Liam in.

"I'm so glad to see you." I catch him around the neck, holding him close. "I'm scared, Liam," I whisper into his ear, and he leans into me.

The hard rain hits my face, and I release him and push at the door, fighting with the wind to get it closed. When I turn, Liam is shaking himself off and the water drops are flying around the room.

I grab my napkin and quickly wipe up what I can. "You will not win his heart by making his room smell like a wet dog." He woofs as I run the fabric over his fur. "We are trying to win his heart; we are trying to win all of their hearts. They are our family now."

Straightening, I put it back on the table then turn and see Liam climbing on the bed.

"I'm not sure that's a good idea," I scold him, but as usual, he chooses to ignore me.

Thunder cracks and shakes the ship, and I jump, landing on the bed next to my protector and pull him close to me. "Just for a little bit," I say as the ship rolls from one side to the other.

My stomach does the same as I watch the dessert slide back and forth across the table.

"Oh God, I'm going to be sick," I gasp, swallowing hard just as the door flies open to show the darkened sky behind the man standing in the doorway. He is outlined when lightning flashes in the sky and he looks every bit the warrior from the cover of that old book. Hair blowing and shirt stuck to him from the rain, he is something to behold.

"Don't you dare throw up on my bed," he grumbles while shoving the door closed behind him.

I swallow again, trying to keep the spicy food down. Mortified, I don't say anything. If I open my mouth, it will be over, no way to stop the inevitable. He frowns when he sees my reaction to another wave and then dashes toward the desk sitting in the corner. I swallow again and let my eyes close, trying to block out the movement. His hand on my shoulder, gentle but firm, makes me open them once again, and I see him.

He's kneeling beside the bed, bucket in hand, and there's no mistaking the concern and worry on his face.

"Too many waves," I mumble through clenched teeth.

"I know, pet." His voice is deep and his hand smooths circles over my back.

"I don't think I can be a pirate," I gasp out as another wave rolls the boat. I can feel it dip low on its side just as I lose my fight.

I heave and heave until sweat coats my skin. All the while, he holds my hair back as I clutch the bucket. I don't even remember grabbing it but I currently hold it like it's a life line. I know soon my embarrassment will take over but for now, I just continue to throw up, grateful he is here.

Hours later, I'm curled on my side and he is still with me, curled around me. His hand is rubbing gently over my finally calm stomach. The storm still rages, but having him by me has calmed me. Maybe it is simply I have nothing left to heave up.

He has hummed softly ever since he got me to lie down, some song I don't recognize, but it is beautiful, somehow reminding me of the forest. He has drawn my mind away from the rolling, and I'm focused on the flashes of light and the sound of the rain on the panes of the window.

"Better?" His breath is hot against my neck and the hairs of his beard tickle the sensitive skin.

"A little. Thank you."

"For what? Getting you a bucket? That was mostly to save my bed," he jokes.

I shift, turning toward him some, and look at his face, taking in every minute detail.

"You held my hair," I say and instantly I can see he doesn't get it. "You stayed and held my hair."

"I know." His brows draw down, and I smile at him.

"I'd kiss you but…" I put my fingers in front of my mouth.

He watches me while he brings his face down, and I melt when he presses his lips to my forehead, and they stay there as I draw in a deep breath.

When he moves back, I just stare at him and I can feel tears spring into my eyes but I try to blink them away.

"I'm sorry," he mumbles and leaps from the bed before I can even try to explain.

He's out the door before I can get myself up. I sit on the bed, swaying slightly as black spots swim before my eyes. I'm still there when the door opens and a young man comes in carrying a jug. He sits it on the table beside the bed and then lays a twig and a pot of sea salt beside it.

"The captain thought you'd like to freshen up," he says without making eye contact and then grabs the bucket and practically flees the room. I stare after him long after the door is closed then look down at the things he left.

It's everything I need to clean the residue from my teeth and mouth and clean the sweat from my body. I pick up the twig and rub my thumb over the end, flaring it out, then dip it in the water before tapping it into the salt.

I scrub my teeth and inside of my mouth, repeating the tap and dip over and over until all I can taste is the strangely minty salt. Finally, I rinse one last time, lay the twig down, and pick up the salt container, bringing it up to my nose.

The smell of mint is stronger than the actual flavor. I've got to ask who makes it.

Putting it back, I look around and see a small basin on the floor near his wardrobe. I take one more steadying breath and then I stand. I stay put for a moment and then cross to get the bowl before making my way back to the table where the dessert still sits staring at me, daring me to take a bite.

"Not today." I shake my head, pushing it well away. I don't even want to smell the sweetness. "Maybe not ever."

The water is warm but it is cooling quickly, so I glance at the door as I strip. My clothes fall in a heap at my feet, and I pick up the rag that was with the basin and pick up the jug of water in my other hand. Pouring the water into the basin, I glance around as I sit it back on the table.

Soap. Laying the rag on the edge of the basin, I turn around and look at the corner where I grabbed the bowl. There is a small wooden crate, and I cross to it and see a misshapen chunk of soap in it, along with a brush and a few other things. I grab the brush and the soap then go back to the table.

Placing the items down on the table, I grab the rag once again then dunk it in the water. I wash my skin, removing the sweat and grime from the last few days. It had been a few days, but with so much going on, I hadn't even thought of it. I'm sure I had begun to stink.

I rinse the soap from my skin and pick up another piece

of fabric to scrub myself dry. My skin is pink when I finally finish, and I gasp as the door flies open.

Cyder stands there frozen until he hears steps behind him. Before I can blink or cover even an inch of my skin, he slams the door shut and locks it.

We both stare, our bodies locked in place. My skin grows pinker as I reach behind me and pull up a pillow, which was the first thing my fingers touched. I bring it around and cover myself, entirely too late, but it does allow for him to blink, and then the spell is broken.

"I'm sorry," he mumbles, then pauses. "Actually, no. I'm not sorry at all but for God's sake, woman, lock the door the next time. I'd hate to have to kill a member of my crew for seeing you."

I shiver at the tone and promise in it. He wasn't kidding; he would kill anyone who saw me. It's both terrifying and exhilarating. I step around the table, the pillow still held to me.

"I'm sorry. You ran before I could explain." I reach him and press close, letting his body hold the pillow between us. "The tears were for your sweetness, your kindness." I reach up and touch his cheek, reveling in the silky softness of his beard. "You have stolen a piece of my heart."

His eyes widen at my words, and then his body relaxes. I know then how worried he was.

"I..." He stopped and looked at me, really studied me. His eyes roam over my face, memorizing it.

I feel his hand move over the bare skin at my hip, lightly sliding around while moving up to my waist.

"I realize now I have no clothes aboard your ship," I whisper, loving the hunger that blazes bright in his eyes.

"You are tempting me to do things we have all agreed to wait for." His fingers tighten on my skin.

"I don't remember being present for this agreement," I

murmur while rising up. I let my lips feather over the skin on his chest along his collar bone.

"Pet, please, I will not disrespect my brothers," he growls but doesn't push me away.

"Fine," I growl right back as I turn, letting the pillow fall. I saunter slowly to the bed and slide under the covers. He groans and I hide a smile. "Your decision... Pet." I look back over my shoulder at him.

He is holding the pillow in front of him, and I let my gaze drift down to what he is possibly hiding.

He throws the pillow across the room, and it lands at my side. Cyder spins and jerks the door open, slamming it behind him to leave me alone in his bed. I wait as long as I can before sleep drags me to darkness.

I wake hours later; darkness is fading and heat surrounds me. His heat.

CHAPTER FOUR
CYDER

*S*he is awake.

Not moving, breathing as slowly and shallowly as she can, but she is awake. Her body tensed slightly when she felt me behind her.

"Morning," I say the word low and let my breath heat her skin even more.

"I didn't hear you when you came back. I didn't feel you come to me." She sounds petulant.

"I was quiet. You needed to rest." I kiss the skin just at the base of her neck.

"Where did you go?"

I don't speak. Instead, I point at the foot of the bed. Her head turns, and a small gasp escapes as she pushes up. Her hand reaches out for the clothes I had draped over the footboard, clothes that I had pulled from one of my treasure chests. When I had started packing them away some years ago, I didn't know why but I thought they might be needed at some point.

Maybe it was a hope or a wish but whatever it might have been, I'm thankful for it now. The joy on her face is worth the looks the items had garnered from my men and my brothers.

The clothes are fitting of a queen—dresses, pants, and shirts all in the softest, most brilliantly colored fabrics. Some are from a time before, but others I had made from the pictures in books. I had found a woman who could create anything if you could bring her the materials. She didn't let me down when I showed her the pictures from the books.

Months later, she had gotten word to me to pick up my order.

Reyna is kneeling, clutching the sheet to her front, but her delectable ass is bare to me, and I hunger to run my hands over it. I desire to grip it tight and drag her back to me.

"Cyder?"

When I look up, she is grinning. Minx.

"Sorry, your ass distracted me." I won't hide my desire from her.

"I said thank you and they are too much." Her fingers stroke the fabric, proving her words a lie. "Where did they come from?"

"I found some here and there. Others I had made." I raise up, bracing on my elbows.

"Made for who?" She can't hide the hint of jealousy in her voice.

"You."

"Me?" Her eyes widen and a smile blooms over her face.

"It seems so. I didn't have a person in mind but I had them made anyway. And I'm almost positive they will fit you as if they were sewn for you."

She turns around and comes back to me, the sheet between us but once again her butt bare, and this time, I don't stop myself. I grab it and pull her against me tighter, letting her feel what she's done to me.

Her moan makes me harder.

She slides up my body, and it's my turn to groan.

Our lips meet in a crash of hunger. She kisses like she is starving, and I let her feast. I kiss her until we are both gasping, but neither of our hungers are sated even slightly. The kisses only stoke the flames higher.

"Reyna," I murmur against her now swollen lips. "We must stop or I won't be able to."

"We keep having the same conversation, but I understand your honor, your promise." She pushes up some, keeping the sheet pulled to her. "I will stop but I need to put more than this sheet between us, and you need to let go of my ass."

She grins as I flex my fingers once before letting them drop to the mattress. It is the one thing I can do to keep my honor. She is bringing us to our knees, and we are all happy to be there, her willing subjects.

She grabs a dress at the end of the bed, and I let my head fall back as the sheet drops. Closing my eyes, I try and fail not to picture her. Seconds draw out to minutes and what seems like hours later, I feel her draw near.

"You can open your eyes, Cyder," she whispers near my head.

I wait a beat then do just what she suggested. She stands before me, looking regal.

My Queen.

A sharp whistle cuts through the air, and she turns her head toward the door before looking back at me. I have already flung my legs over the edge of the bed and I'm pushing up to my feet.

"You slept in your clothes," she murmurs, and I don't understand the look on her face.

"Of course." I frown as the look deepens and she blinks rapidly.

I stop trying to figure it out and step around her so I can

grab my boots. Leaning over, I pull on one then the other before I straighten. She is standing right in front of me when I do.

Before I can react, she grabs my face firmly but gently and pulls it down, kissing me. It's different than the heated kisses from moments ago. I think I might like this one more. It says something that I understand about as much as the look on her face but I can feel it's important.

I kiss her back and try my best to tell her how I feel, tell us both, since I'm not sure what this feeling is.

We break apart at the sound of another whistle.

"Come on, pet. Someone is needing to speak to us, I fear." I take her hand and lead her out onto the deck.

The morning has dawned clear and the sky is beautiful but it has nothing on her in the dress. The reaction by the crew that are on deck says they feel the same thing. It is different shades of dark blue, the darkest almost black, and it has silver threads stitched throughout. All she is lacking is the crown.

My brothers have positioned themselves in front of us and dropped anchor. I nod at my first mate and he does the same, lowering our sails, which have taken a beating in the storm.

Fallon swings over as soon as we are stopped. My crew has brought us perpendicular to the others, our port side along their afts. The others follow closely behind him and they all freeze when they see her. Looking beyond them, I see crews from each ship gather at their rails, looking at us. At her.

She is beaming, oblivious of the uproar she is causing.

"Reyna." Fallon nods his head once, and she dances over to him, twirling, showing off the dress.

"Isn't it beautiful." It's a statement as she glances back at me.

"Yes, it is." Hagen looks her up and down, not even trying to hide the lust in his gaze.

She blushes but returns his look with one almost as hungry. Wilder watches and I see his eyes narrow before he looks at me. I jerk my head, beckoning him and Fallon to my side while she gets spun around again by Hagen. Her breathless laughter fills the morning.

Glancing around, I want to laugh at the mooning the men are doing but honestly, I feel for the poor bastards. She is the perfect mixture of sweet and sassy, inducing a myriad of emotions. I can tell all my brothers want to both protect her and ravish her. The crews are ready to fall on a sword for her.

Lash is the last to join us and he pauses on the rail.

I haven't seen him seem so lost in many years and never for this reason.

Reyna notices him, frozen on the rail, and slows her spinning, then pulls away from Hagen, who starts to join the rest of us.

"Do you like it? Cyder was kind enough to give it to me."

I'm happy she left out what I told her about having it made for her.

"You are breathtaking." Lash's voice is reverent. "A true queen."

She holds up a hand and he takes it, jumping down. He lands directly in front of her, inches separating them. She stares up into his face, and for a split second, I hate him for his beautiful face. Glancing from side to side, I feel slightly ashamed because I see none of my envy on my brothers' faces.

"They make quite the couple," I hear someone murmur from behind us and look back to see at least five of my crew standing and staring.

"I hate that they aren't wrong," Hagen grumbles but a small smile is on his face.

"Same, brother." Fallon chuckles.

They jest, but I spin on my heels to head back to my quarters. I can feel the others' eyes on me and I flip my middle finger at them. Hagen bellows and I can picture Wilder shaking his head solemnly while Fallon frowns.

It is Fallon's steps I hear start to follow me.

I throw myself on the couch and wait for the others to join me. Fallon is first, of course, and he glances around, taking in everything from the placement of the bed to the bucket beside it.

"She had a rough night." I don't elaborate, for there is no need.

"How was your night?" He asks as Wilder and Hagen join us.

"Long."

Hagen cackles this time. This is the most I've heard him laugh in our lives.

"Shut up, idiot," I growl, and he just laughs more.

"What's the matter, Cyder? You couldn't steal any kisses?" He snickers, but his eyes are extremely watchful.

"Not the problem." Now they all frown, and it's my turn to smile.

They wait and I draw out the silence, loving the glances they keep throwing at her out on deck. She and Lash are doing some slow dance, and I realize his gold tunic and dark pants look like they were made to complement her dress.

"They look like the paintings in some of the books." Wilder's voice is low and filled with emotion.

"He is just as beautiful as she is," Fallon agrees, and I feel that ugly emotion start to churn.

"I don't know if I can do this," I admit, and they all look back at me.

"Did you not connect with her?" Wilder questions, but it's Hagen that looks at me with understanding.

I'm surprised when he moves to join me. "Can we have a moment, brothers?" He asks, but his tone doesn't really offer the choice for them to deny his request.

Both just turn and leave, shutting the door behind them. We both sit in silence, listening to the sounds of laughter just beyond the wood.

"We aren't like them. Never have been," Hagen starts as he drags his gaze back to me. "That fact is neither good nor bad. It is just a fact."

I open my mouth to argue on that point, but he shakes his head.

"Wilder will have no problem sharing her love, and she will need his safety and calm," he continues before pausing once again, glancing at the door. "Fallon, well, she already loves him, whether she knows it or not. They bonded in the cave he woke in and in the darkness of her despair."

I couldn't argue with his observations; it is what he does.

"She is drawn to my darkness. It calls to the wildness in her." He watches for my reaction.

I sigh. "I know."

"She will be drawn to Lash's brokenness, his need for someone to love the man he keeps protected and hidden. He will draw her need to protect."

Great, now I feel like more of an asshole. "When did you get so goddamn insightful?"

"I always have been; I just don't care to share my thoughts." He shrugs.

"So like I said, I don't know if I can do this. She will have no need for me. She finds me attractive but she will not need me." I sound like a child.

"All the better for you."

"How exactly?" I scoff, spoiling for a fight.

"Because when she comes to you, it will be because she chooses to for no other reason than yourself. I believe it will be you she seeks when she just wants to be Reyna. Not our queen, not our savior, but the woman she was. You are the one she would have chosen for herself."

I stare, at a loss for words, and he laughs, his hand coming out to pat me on the shoulder before he rises. I watch as he walks out the door, leaving it open.

She turns when she hears his steps, and concern clouds her face for a moment as we lock eyes. I smile, trying to reassure her, and she returns it with a tentative one of her own.

Lash is standing behind her, and I nod at him before standing up.

'No sense sitting in here like a child,' I chastise myself.

I stand then and cross to the door, trying to get my emotions under control in the few steps it takes me. Hagen's words are playing over and over in my mind. I would have been the one chosen. As I stand there leaning against the frame, I imagine it.

I can see us together in a home, a house in some village filled with our children and her beast. I can practically smell the food on the stove. I can hear her laughter and the giggles of a child. Before I realize it, my hand is over my heart as it clenches in my chest.

How our lives could have been different if the King hadn't found us.

Of course, life is weird that way. I would have never met her. Or is it that destiny would have brought us all together, no matter what?

Without the King, we would not be who we are. It is our lives that have shaped us. He, no matter how much I hate to admit it, made us the men we are.

"I think we have time," Hagen was saying, the breeze bringing his words to me.

"Time for what?" I push off the door frame and head toward them.

"Repairs. The storm ripped some sails on each of our ships," Fallon responds, looking over at my own sails.

"Do you think I could go ashore? I need to get my feet on solid ground. I know Liam would probably like to run as well." Reyna looks at each of them before focusing on me, a silent plea in her eyes.

"I think that is an excellent idea."

She smiles at my support.

"I could take you," Lash offers quietly.

She turns, and I can tell she's smiling at his offer from the look on his face. "I'd love that."

"It's settled then." Fallon looks at me then the others. "Maybe that beast will get us some more meat."

"I'll get some boats down and have the men fish while we are here, too. Good time to restock the supply, if we can. We don't know what will happen next." I look at the others hard.

Reyna sighs, and I can only imagine the thoughts that might be going through her head. She starts toward the cabin, trailing her fingers over each of us. That small motion, that act of inclusion, settles something in me.

Hagen was right, in a way, but I understand now that that touch is her choosing us all. I look back at my brothers, and they are watching me.

"What?" I wait for the smirks, but they never come.

"That was a beautiful dress, perfect for her." Wilder looks over at the closed door.

"Fitting of a queen," Fallon agrees.

"Oh. Yes, I thought it highlighted her skin," I agree and instantly regret it as they all begin to grin. "Oh, wipe those fucking grins off your faces. She has us all…" I wave my hand around making sure to encompass all the crews still watching the door. "ALL… wrapped around her finger."

"True." They all nod at Hagen's laughed word while also looking at the men standing near. Hagen frowns then levels all of them with a glare. "Get to work!"

They start to scurry on every ship, sails being drawn down and repairs getting started.

"Can we talk about what we are going to do about the fleet of ships that are hunting us?"

"The King has hunted us for years." Hagen shrugs, ignoring the pain from the fresh wound in his leg as he limps away to the stairs.

We all join him, standing close so we can discuss our next steps.

"My lady."

We turn and see Reyna standing just outside the door. She's now wearing pants and a shirt that hug her curves. The image of her from last night invades my mind and my cock hardens.

"So, can we still go to shore?" She asks when none of us move.

"Yes. Of course." Lash holds out his hand, and she crosses to him to take it. "Let's get over to the... ship."

I look over at Hagen, who is literally biting his lips to keep from laughing. Even Wilder's lips are twitching at Lash's omission of his ship's name.

"Yes, head on over to the Howling Lust," Wilder drawls.

Reyna bows her head, hiding the grin on her face. Lash sighs but steps away from us, pulling her with him.

"Liam," she calls from the rail, and we all watch as the beast races toward them, leaping at the last minute and soaring to the other ship.

"Shit."

"I don't know what he is, but that is no ordinary dog." Wilder frowns, watching as Liam rushes back and forth, waiting for his mistress to reach his side.

"She's more, so it makes sense he is too." Fallon leans against the rail.

I have a moment of feeling like I wish I was more.

"She was sent to us, and we were sent to her," Wilder says under his breath.

"Get out of my head, brother." I glare at him.

"Don't need to be in it. Your doubts are written all over your face, for those of us who know you." Fallon straightens. "We all have them." He looks at Lash catching Reyna as she jumps from the rail of the Lust. "Our brother most of all.

CHAPTER FIVE
LASH

I can feel their eyes on us. I hold her gently as I set her on the deck. Liam pushes into us, shoving us closer together, and she laughs. It is beautiful and brings thoughts of a time before the darkness.

I know what people see when they look at me. I've worked very hard to make sure they see exactly what I want them to, but it's not me. I wear this persona like a shield. It, the mask, protects me. I became this version of Lash long ago in the darkness of his rooms.

"Lash?" Her voice is soft, like she's trying to calm a wild animal.

"Sorry. Just thinking. Shall we get going?" She nods, letting me change the subject.

"Yes." She raises her brows while running her hand over Liam's haunches.

"Just let me grab some lunch from Cook," I tell her before turning toward the stairs.

I leave her looking around the deck, smiling at every crewman that finds a reason to wander close. There seem to be quite a few. My brothers are right; she is enchanting all of them. All of us.

Word must have spread because Damon is waiting with food packed and ready to go.

"Thank you, Damon." I pause with my hand on the small crate.

"I filled it with every treat I've had ready in case she came to visit us." Damon taps the edge of the crate while looking at me. "I will not let those other degenerates beat me with their hash."

"Rightly so. No way they could ever dream of coming close to your skill." I stroke his delicate ego.

Damon wasn't a pirate by nature. No, I had found him at a restaurant during one of my trips while bartering deals for us. He had been cooking for people that didn't appreciate his talents. After dinner, I had gone and spoken to him, made promises to get him exotic ingredients. He had agreed to come aboard, and I had fulfilled my promise. Every stop, I found things for him to make into delicious dishes—spices and different meats. My men and I ate very well. Some time later, I had found out about Damon's family. Generation after generation had passed down skills and knowledge that had been learned before the battle, before the world was almost destroyed.

"We must find you a wife, Damon, so you can have a son or daughter to teach your secrets," I murmur as I draw a deep breath, savoring the aromas.

"Are all women welcome now, sir?" He looks like he doesn't believe it.

"I wouldn't say that but for you and your skills, I might make an exception," I admit.

"I'll keep it in mind but I think maybe one woman on these ships is enough, especially this woman." Damon looks beyond me, and I turn but see no one. "She is beautiful and special."

"That she is." I sigh. "How much so, we still don't know."

"I watched her on Captain Cyder's ship, twirling in the sunlight; it was like something from a dream." He sounds wistful.

"Magical, to be sure," I answer and then pick up the crate. "Thank you again. I'll make sure to tell her this is just a sample of what you can do."

He grins, but I can tell exactly how much the thought pleases him. I leave him there looking smug and start down the hall.

She is talking to one of the crew when I reach the top of the stairs, leaning close to hear whatever it is he is saying. I watch as she points and he nods. I draw close, and the man straightens and takes a small step away.

"Captain," he defers, and she turns toward me with a smile on her face, cheeks pink with excitement.

"Are you ready?" I ask as I lead her to the other side of the ship, where the dingy is waiting.

"Yes." She looks at me and the trust in her eyes just about brings me to my knees.

I lock the picture away in my mind. She won't look at me the same way when she learns all of my secrets. And she will find out. There will be no way to hide certain aspects of me if we become close.

My muscles tighten just at the thought of having to tell her, to explain to her. The shame makes my anger flare, and I fight to shove it away. I can't ruin my time with her. Today, I will wear my mask tightly over my scars.

"Great. Just let me get in first." She nods as I step over the edge and then settle the crate before standing up and holding up my hand for her.

She takes it, and I savor the feel of her smooth skin

against mine. She jumps down with no fear, or her need to be off the water just overshadows it.

The hound is next, and his huge weight rocks us on the ropes as the men start to lower us. They get us down quickly, and I grab the oars and start to move us to the shore. As soon as the boat hits the shore, she is up and out of the boat, her feet getting wet as she splashes through the water with Liam hot on her heels.

I get out and pull at the rope, dragging it a little farther on shore then wrap it around a tree washed up on the rocks. Going back to grab the crate, I look out at the ships, watching as the sails are lowered.

"Do you think we could go farther in, into the forest?" She calls from just at the edge of the trees.

"I don't see why not. Lead the way," I call out, expecting her to continue on her way but she doesn't.

She waits. For me. I reach her side in moments, and she links her arm with mine.

We walk into the forest together.

She leads me deep into the trees, where the branches and leaves filter the sun. Random shafts highlight the blueish tints in her hair. Every few moments, she glances up at me. I don't know what she's looking for but I hope she finds it.

The others have more to offer her. I have my looks, my talents, so to speak, but she seems uninterested in those. I let her take me deeper and deeper, far away from the shore and the ships.

The sound of gentle water draws her attention, and she changes direction, heading straight to it. The sound of limbs breaking draws my eyes to our left, and I see the dog running straight at us before he quickly shifts directions, his nose to the ground.

"He'll bring something back." She's grinning as he disappears.

Her steps begin to slow, and I wait for her to decide if this is the perfect spot. Finally, she stops near the stream, a spot both under a tree and in the sunlight.

"This is perfect." Reyna spins in a circle, looking just as beautiful in the pants and shirt as she did in the dress.

"Okay, great."

She pulls the fabric from the crate and flicks it out into the air, letting it spread wide as it drifts down to the ground. Sitting, it's her turn to hold her hand up. Shifting the crate to under my arm, I reach down and let her take my hand and pull me down. As soon as I get settled, she starts to dig into the crate, pulling out all the food that Damon packed.

"Everything looks so good." She places a bowl under her nose, drawing a deep breath. "I can't believe how good you all eat." Her eyes move over each dish.

"Normally, we don't. Not that we eat bad, but Damon and the other cooks are trying to win you over with their best dishes."

She sits back and looks it all over again. "They shouldn't do anything special for me." A protest.

"You are our chosen. You will be, are already, their queen. They want to please you," I tell her then let my voice drop. "I want to please you."

Her gaze whips up to mine, and I level her with the look that has had women begging for me to take them home. Reyna's eyes flair but she doesn't say or do anything. Instead, she leans back away from me.

"So, you are the one that forges new deals for you all," she asks, and the subject confuses me.

"Yes."

"Lash." She smiles but it's a little sad, and my stomach clenches a little. "I want to get to know you."

She emphasizes the last word.

"I am an open book," I assure her.

"I doubt it." Her words are said low as she turns her face to look at the water.

"What do you want to know?" Inside I'm screaming, praying she doesn't ask about the scars or anything from that time.

"What's something you love? The others each have something that's special to them. Like Wilder and his books. Hagen has weapons. Fallon, his carving. What do you have?"

The question seems innocent enough but for me, not so much. "What does Cyder have?"

"He loves the people that he thinks he comes from, their culture. The music and art, everything as far as I could tell." She doesn't turn to look at me, just keeps looking out at the forest and the stream.

What do I have? What do I have to offer her? That's what the question is really asking.

"If you don't, it's fine."

I can hear the truth, but there is something more in her tone. Something that makes me swallow hard.

"Reyna?" She turns now eyes locking with mine. "I'm going to fail this test. I'm not like the others."

"This isn't a test, Lash." I don't believe her and I can tell she knows. I'm ready for her to shut me out, but instead, she grabs my hand. "Let's just eat then. I'd hate to waste this food and I'm starving. I didn't have a good night."

I feel relief but also I'm ashamed that I've let her down. She starts opening different containers, bringing each to her nose before setting it back down on the fabric.

Just as we are about to take our first bite, a howl rings through the forest and her eyes move from side to side, searching. Another howl and she whips her head to the right, looking at where the land begins to rise up into a cliff.

"He is on the trail of something." She sounds sure, and I

believe her. "He will bring something back for certain; he never loses his prey."

It is a good piece of information to have about her protector.

"Reyna." I say her name to draw her attention back to me as I hold out a plate with samplings of all of Damon's treats.

"Thank you." She takes it and my muscles tighten with just the touch of her fingers on mine.

We eat but the food is practically tasteless to me as I watch her enjoy hers. It is a seduction, one that I'm positive she doesn't even know that she is doing. She is just enjoying herself.

She fills her plate again, now picking the favorites of Damon's samples. Her gaze keeps straying to the desserts which she hasn't tasted.

"Damon was working in a small restaurant when I found him. The techniques and recipes were passed down from his family. Apparently, his ancestor had been a famous chef who had traveled the world. She had survived the disaster, created a family in the aftermath, and taught her children her skills. And so it went until Damon. He is the last of her long line. I told him we needed to get him a wife so he can have a child to teach." I fall silent, and she is smiling.

"I wonder if he would teach me some of them?"

I wonder about her smile; it seems like it isn't about Damon at all, but I can't figure out why it wouldn't be.

"I'm sure he would," I answer while holding out a small pot of chocolate cream.

The chocolate is very rare, we traded for it the last time we were in the South Seas.

"What is it?" She reaches out and sticks just the tip of a finger in the little pot.

"Chocolate. It's extremely hard to come by." I watch as she

brings the small taste to her mouth, her tongue flicking out to lick it off.

"Oh, my. It's delicious." She stares longingly at the pot in my hand. "I've never tasted anything like it.

"Damon was ecstatic when we found it. He rarely uses his stash."

"I would use it all the time."

I pick up a spoon and hold it out beside the pot. "He made it for you." I think for a moment she would argue, but she snatches them from my fingers and I laugh.

"Sorry. I would fight you for this."

I hold up my hands in surrender as I lean back against the boulder behind me. She takes small amounts on the spoon, savoring each taste.

Scooping more out, she looks over at me watching her, then scoots over until her side is touching mine. I put my arm around her shoulders, letting her relax back against me. She surprises me by holding up the spoon, but I take it, the smooth creaminess covering my tongue.

Without thought, I grip her chin gently and force her head up and back, turning her mouth toward me and kissing her just as her eyes widen. I kiss her, tasting the chocolate on her tongue as she opens for me, and I force the kiss to deepen.

I kiss her like a starving man and maybe I am.

I pour my loneliness in the kiss, silently begging her to save me. But that isn't fair, I shouldn't put that kind of responsibility on her, but I've tried. So instead I thrust my tongue deeper, rubbing it against hers as I hear a soft noise. Then her hand reaches back, her fingers curling into my hair and pulling me to her even more.

We kiss like this until we are both breathless, until my need for her is overwhelming my control. I end it by pulling back just a bit, keeping my lips right against hers as I run my tongue over their plumpness before moving to the side and dragging my tongue over her jaw.

Her moan is almost my undoing, but a twig snapping has me raising my head, my eyes scanning the area around us. I see nothing as she straightens, her own eyes quartering the area just like my own.

"Do you see anything?" Her words are whispered low.

"No. It could be nothing."

"It could've been Liam," she suggests, but I'm almost positive that sound wasn't made by the beast coming to check on his mistress.

"Maybe." She looks over at me, and I can see she heard my disbelief. "I don't know, something seems..." I trail off, my head shaking.

I can't put my finger on it, but something is off.

CHAPTER SIX
HAGEN

*T*hey've been gone for a few hours, and I keep looking at the shore, my gut churning. Something is wrong.

Looking away, I try to check on the others but I don't see them. Fallon and Wilder have finally left their decks, but I can hear Cyder calling out orders, his voice tight with either frustration or anger.

I'd wager that it was frustration; I think we are all feeling a bit of it. The whole situation has us all on edge, not just my brothers. The crews are wound tight as well. It's not just Reyna's presence; it's the unrelenting pursuit by the King.

The King chasing us is nothing new, but he has grown more determined to catch us. I pause, looking up at the sky, at the birds flying overhead, and let my mind drift just like they are. Something has changed.

Lowering my face, I look around, the "something" is more than Reyna, although she is at the center of it all. I don't think he knows we have her, the girl he's been searching for, but he knows she is real. I don't think the man that told

Wilder about the girl and her importance would have told the King.

So who did?

It's been niggling at the back of my mind since we looked at the chest, since she told us about the letter. Someone has been guiding us to her, and maybe her to us. But that means maybe we aren't the only ones to have a guardian angel helping.

I've played it all over and over in my mind. I've examined every memory since I met Fallon. For an instant, the darkness of the hold of the King's ship darkens my vision.

Who have I seen?

Who was out of place?

Who was always there?

Who was there with no reason to be?

All very good questions that I have no answer for. I whistle, three short bursts of sound, and wait. My brothers all join me within minutes.

"Hagen?" Fallon frowns at me, reflecting my own worry.

"What is it?" Wilder asks as soon as Fallon finishes.

Cyder remains silent, just watching. We all have our roles. I protect them.

"Think back. Do you remember ever seeing someone on his ship that seemed out of place?" I watch their faces, watching as they do as I ask.

Their eyes move almost like they are watching the memories and maybe they are, a way to separate themselves from the pain of them. It isn't something I'm capable of. I feel each blow of the whip, the fist, hell, even the words.

He was very good at what he did, finding our weaknesses and exploiting them. What did we need? I shake my head, swallowing hard and trying to pull myself back to the present.

The words.

They often play on a loop through my head. We all got the beatings, but for me, it was the deprivation that made me who I am. He knew as soon as he found me what I craved, knew I would all but kill myself to get it. So he never offered it.

Which only made me try harder to get it. I did things, horrible things, to hear the words he never spoke. My teeth grind.

"Hagen?" Fallon is watching me closely when I look up at him.

"Sorry." I don't need to say more, for they already know.

"I can't think of anyone," he responds to my question then looks at the others, and they all nod. "Although I can remember times where he was locked away in his cabin."

"What are you thinking, Hagen?" Wilder is watching just me. I can see his brain whirling, trying to process the information, filling in gaps, trying to understand what I've figured out.

"Well, I think someone, the person that the letter mentioned, has been nudging us toward Reyna for a long time, maybe our whole lives." They all nod. "The King has been chasing us harder and searching for her. I can't help but wonder if someone is also nudging him."

Cyder clenches his fists and paces away. Wilder and Fallon look at each other then back at me, and I see the anger boiling there in their gazes.

Cyder stomps back. "Our whole lives? This person has watched and allowed…" He trails off and stomps away again, jumping on the rail then leaping across to his own ship. The sound of his cabin door slamming is loud, even from here.

"I don't disagree with his thoughts," I say as I turn toward my own cabin. I can hear the others following behind me.

"Maybe not our whole lives." Wilder is the first to speak.

"Surely, this person wouldn't have let him...let us..." He stutters.

I feel his hurt. Wilder and Lash were the more gentle of us all, small and seemingly delicate boys. Lash was beautiful, hell, he still is, and the things he suffered... Wilder could read, and that saved him some of the worst treatment. But that small difference didn't in any way save him.

So many broken and destroyed by his depravity, his absolute evil. His whole crew, the ones on his personal ship, are all just like him. Made by him. Some of the captured boys, most really, were sent to the others' ships. Those were the lucky ones.

We were special, chosen to serve on his ship. I have often wondered what he saw in us, how he knew he could break us. Because no matter what we chose to do, since we were thrown away like trash, we were broken. It was the island and our fight for survival that shaped us into who we are now.

We are a tapestry of our scars, both physical and mental.

I have a tattered tapestry I found in the city hanging in my quarters, the delicate threads woven together to form a beautiful picture of a world lost long ago. Sometimes I stare at it, trying to picture a life within the world that they have created. I can't.

"No. I don't think our whole lives, but maybe for a while now. He or they could be the ones that protected the city, who put five ships at the dock. Hell, they could have made sure we got there. Or maybe when we arrived, they started watching. We didn't see the ships right away." I shrug.

"You think they watched as we recovered and put ships for us there after we were deemed worthy?" Fallon frowns at his own words.

"I don't know. I just had the thought that we aren't the only ones being guided. He is getting bolder, more desperate, and there has to be a reason. I think that reason is someone whispering to him, pointing him in the general direction, which means whoever the person is that's helping doesn't know exactly where Reyna was or is." I voice my thoughts.

"So is the King tracking her, us, or the pull of whatever we are now searching for?" Wilder glances at us both.

"That is the question, isn't it?" I look out at the shore.

"You think we need to get to one of the safe harbors?" Fallon asks then falls silent, waiting for my answer.

"I don't know. In port, we are sitting ducks but running in open water, he's got the numbers on us." I sigh. "I think I wish we had more friends."

"Let's try to make a plan. If he is chasing us to get Reyna, we need to be prepared." Fallon stands just as a whistle cuts through the air.

I stand and turn to look at Cyder's ship anchored behind us. His crewman is high in the crows nest looking behind them, and Cyder runs from his quarters, sliding to a stop to look up at his man. The man holds up his arm pointing south.

Shading my eyes with my hand, I look and can just see sails.

"Fuck. They found the channel. Get the sails back up! I don't fucking care if they are ready or not!" I scream at the crew.

Fallon and Wilder each start to run. Fallon whistles to his own crew as he pauses to yell at Lash's crew to make ready. My eyes turn toward the shore just as Fallon looks back. His head shakes, and I punch the railing.

"He will keep her safe. We have to leave them or they will swarm the forest looking for her," he orders and I nod curtly, knowing he's right but hating it.

Just as I turn to start yelling orders, another whistle echoes and I look behind The Rising Dragon once more, where another set of sails is now in view. The channel is too narrow for us to maneuver to fight. We must run, and Cyder is in my position. His ship doesn't have the guns I have.

"GO!" His deep voice rings out, and I lock eyes with him. "I will follow after I slow them some."

The Dragon has her port side facing them, and I hear him order the gun doors open. By the time I turn back to my own crew, I see Lash's crew has their anchor up and sails open, but their eyes are on the forest, faces tense with anger. They do not wish to leave their captain.

"He will know where to go," I yell at them just as his ship starts to move.

We have plans and backup plans that they will make their way to us. Lash will hear the cannons and know to run. They have the beast and at least a single gun.

"Get us underway. NOW!" I yell, even though my crew began doing just that as soon as the first sails were spotted.

"If you are watching, if you are listening, help would be appreciated," I whisper to the wind, praying whoever has gotten us all in this mess is paying attention.

As our ships all begin to move two across, since that is all the channel will allow, I watch behind us. Cyder should have started to follow but he hasn't, and I frown as I look to my right. Fallon is already watching and as I watch him, his mouth opens and I hear a gut-wrenching "NO." I whip my head back and see men running from the treeline, and some have already entered the water.

The crew sees at the same time and the sails are unfurled, helping to swing the boat around. We watch tense as men start up their ropes even as they rush to raise the anchors completely from the waters. Cannons are fired, shouts can be heard, and we watch helplessly, too far away to stop what is happening.

The ship starts to finally move toward us as I can just

make out a tangle of men falling from the side. Then, one by one, those that had just boarded left alive jump into the water.

"What the fuck is happening?" I ask no one but I look at Fallon once more; he has a telescope to his eye and his face is white. "Fallon?" I yell. "Get my glass!" I yell to the boy close to me, and he runs like the devil is on his heels.

It's in my hands in moments and I look, focusing on the area Fallon is watching. "Fuck." I raise the glass and look at the ships they have slowed. "They got what they wanted."

Boots hit my deck hard, and I look over to see Fallon striding toward me. "They have him."

Fear's cold fingers tighten around my heart.

"They will kill him," I growl.

"No, they want information. They won't kill him, they will torture him first." His voice is low, an anger boiling in his face that I've only seen a few times in our life.

We've all been tortured, but nothing like what Cyder is about to go through.

"Fuck. Fuck. Fuck." My fist hits wood after every word.

I want to kill someone. I want to kill the King. I want to kill every motherfucking one of them. I have had the desire since I was a boy, but now, now this is something altogether different. A new beast has been awakened.

"Get to your ship, brother. We go to Green Cove." It is the closest of our rendezvous spots, a place we can resupply and form a plan of attack.

Fallon nods and does just that, leaving me to my rage. My crew gives me a wide berth as I make my way to my quarters. Jack is waiting by my door.

"They are following without their captain," he mutters.

"As they should," I bark.

He says nothing more as he follows me inside. "To Green

Cove then, sir?" I nod without looking up from the map that is spread on my table.

"Jack, this is about to get ugly, so warn the crew." I glance up as he nods then turns to leave.

Pausing, he looks back at me. "We'll get him, sir."

"Don't make promises you don't know will be kept." He flinches slightly at my harshness but nods before leaving me to my map and anger.

I study the routes, the possible ways they might try to box us in as we move through the channel. How long had we been in before they had somehow found the opening? Is the fleet behind them or has it gone around? Hundreds of questions filter through my mind as I look at the map.

I'm staring at one of the waterways when a drop hits the paper. A tear or sweat? I don't know at first, but then another follows and I realize it's a tear. I scrub at my face, pushing the fear down, pushing away memories of us clinging to one another broken. It is the only way to survive and to save him.

Cyder and I are alike, both hard and distant, still unable to trust because of the things not only done to us but that we did to others. Our brothers never crossed the line, trying to win that thing the King withheld, but we did. We carried out orders, did things that killed parts of us. Those things are our shame; they are why we keep ourselves separate.

My fist hits the table once again.

"Focus, you miserable fuck," I growl at myself. "Think."

I slap my head, trying to dislodge any thoughts stuck behind the memories.

"First thing, get to the rendezvous. Find Reyna and Lash. Save Cyder." *Save Cyder. Save Cyder. Save Cyder.* I say it over and over in my head.

I love Lash and care for Reyna, but Cyder is different. Cyder is in more danger. He will be killed because he will never talk, he would never give us up. Because of his loyalty, he will be taken apart, one cut, one punch, one broken bone at a time.

I need to get word to our friends, our allies. Sitting, I pull paper over and pick up a pencil. I write out six short, concise notes then tear the paper into small pieces that I roll up before I push up and walk out.

"Thomas!" I shout as I walk out of my quarters into the sunlight on the deck.

Boots pound across the smooth wood of the deck, heralding his quick arrival. "Sir." His breath is huffing in and out of his mouth.

"Take these to the birds and send them out. Let me know the moment you get a response." I hold out my hand, and he takes the notes. "Lives depend on your birds, Thomas."

"They won't let you down, sir." He thumps his chest with his fist as he spins away and he goes as he came—at a dead run.

I watch him until he reaches the roost where his birds wait. They are swift, so our message should reach their destinations before we reach our own. They will return to the roost that is there. I just hope our friends will help us. The time has come for everyone to fight back against the terror that sails the seas with us.

We, my brothers and I, have held him at bay as best as we could, but he continues to grow stronger. If he gets whatever is buried, the world will burn once more, and we will not survive it this time.

A war is coming but it will be a slaughter if we don't succeed. Cyder must be saved.

Reyna is the queen, and we are her captains.

*C*annons.

The booms sound like thunder and herald a dark storm.

Lash sets me aside and stands in one motion. I surge up, looking around us. I see nothing and hear nothing. Silence follows the cannon fire, and a loud bark startles me. I jump as Liam bursts through the undergrowth. His hackles are raised, and his keen eyes are focused on the way we came.

"Go check, Liam," I whisper, and he looks at me for a moment before he bounds away. "He has always protected me, always known what to do. He will find out if anyone is after us."

I start to follow the path my friend had taken but I go slower, and Lash is right behind me. We climb up high to a ridge and look out over the treetops to the channel. I gasp, and Lash grabs my hand preventing me from racing forward.

"No."

I turn my face up to his and watch as he studies the ships, his eyes moving over each before his face turns to the right, eyes narrowed for a moment.

"What do you see?" I ask, deciding I need to trust my captain.

"They are retreating." He sounds as if his words confuse him, and I look back at the ships.

I see my captains' ships moving away. Cyder's is last in the line but it is following. I can just barely make out the tiny shapes of two men looking back on Hagen's ship.

"Oh God." Lash's words are low, and his voice is tight with so much emotion as his fingers tighten around mine, crushing the bone.

"What?" My own eyes scan, but I don't see what has upset him.

"In the water. They have Cyder." His finger points, and I can just see them reaching the side of a ship. I can just make out a shock of red hair against the near black of the ship.

"We must get to him. Help him. Save him," I scream, and my voice reverberates off the stone around us.

"We can't. We need to go to the safe harbor. The others will make their way there, and from there, we can save him. The two of us won't survive the King on our own." He turns toward me, gripping my shoulder with his other hand. "He wouldn't want us to sacrifice ourselves on a suicide mission."

I try to pull away but I'm reminded that he is more than a pretty face as he holds me immobile. I'm about to struggle, to try to break free, when I hear a bark. That distant bark pulls my attention from the man holding me. I see a streak of grey that almost blends in with the rocky shore, one that someone who hadn't played hide and seek with an overgrown puppy would overlook. I see Liam flying down the shore at the edge of the trees.

I pull my hand from Lash's and raise both, cupping them around my mouth. I hoot, just three short calls, to let my guardian know I heard him. He will track Cyder.

"What are you doing?" Lash frowns, eyes scanning the water again.

"Letting Liam know I heard him." I don't elaborate. "He's trusting that you will keep me safe for now."

"What do you mean?" He sounds so confused, so I raise my hand and point. He follows the line of my finger.

"He's following them." Incredulous—that's how I'd describe his voice. "Why would he leave you to do that?" He turns his eyes back to me slowly.

"He likes Cyder," I offer and he raises a brow. "Honestly, I don't know why he's tracking him. Maybe he understands how important you all are to me. My mother always said he had been sent to me, so maybe someone commanded him to." I look beyond the man in front of me and watch as the small dot finally disappears from sight. "He will follow as far as he can. He might even try to get to Cyder."

"Try to save Cyder..." His eyes look at the ship growing smaller. "From a ship."

I don't blame him for his disbelief, but Liam has often done the unbelievable. "Don't underestimate his tenacity. He is exactly like a dog with a bone when he's on the trail of something." I let my lips curve slightly.

"You're very funny." He looks back at the ships. His brothers' are almost gone from sight, Cyder's is at the back, moving slightly slower. I can only imagine the turmoil the crew must be in. "We need to get moving."

A howl echoes through the forest but it isn't Liam's. Looking around us, I search but see nothing near us.

"They have found our picnic," Lash whispers. "No going back for the things there." His hand runs over the gun in his waistband that I hadn't noticed before, and then he bends down and pulls not one but two knives from his boot.

Balancing them, he tests the weight of each and then flips one, holding the hilt out to me.

"This one is small but deadly sharp, perfectly balanced, and will be easy for you to handle. Keep it tucked against the inside of your wrist like this." He moves his own along his left wrist, showing me. "Keep it hidden until you are pulled in close, and then stab quick and as many times as you can. Go for the groin, belly, kidneys, throat, or under the arm. Try to cut arteries. You don't want to injure. You want them to bleed out. You want them to die."

I stare at the knife in my hand for a minute before looking up at him, my nerves calmed.

"I've butchered animals but I've never had to defend myself, never had to hurt someone," I tell him because I don't know if I can do what he had described.

"You defended Hagen," he reminds me.

"I did, but that was different, that was..." I pause, not sure what to say, what to call the power that is coming to life within me.

"Magic," he answers for me. "You might not even need the knife, but I feel better with you having it."

He looks out at the water one last time before turning toward the forest. He holds his hand out, and I take it, letting him start us on our journey. We walk in silence until the sun starts to set. I slow when I see a tree with low branches thick with foliage, growing right up against a sheer cliff of rock.

"We should stop here." I turn, looking over at him. "I can make a good shelter here."

He looked around with a small frown on his face.

"Trust me." I turn toward the tree. "Why don't you gather firewood and get a fire started?"

I can feel his eyes on me as I move around the area, gathering leaves and grasses for a bed. He finally starts to move, and I smile, my face turned away from him. He's only gone a few minutes before he returns, his arms full of fallen branches. He breaks them up before placing them in an area I had cleared of debris. Before he starts the fire, he grabs rocks and circles the area to keep the flames contained.

"Have you spent much time on land?" I call over my shoulder.

"Not really. The longest was in the city we found. Before that, it was when I was with my family." His voice grew quiet on the last few words.

"Do you remember them? Your brothers each had some memories, although they also spoke of them fading," I ask as I pull down a branch, using a separate branch to stake it to the ground.

I repeat the process until I've made a cozy shelter just big enough for us.

"I do. Barely." His voice is right by my ear, and I jerk before he wraps his arms around me. "This looks amazing. You've got skills."

I let the subject of his family drop. Like the others, he doesn't want to face memories of things he can't have. I understand. I have my memories, years of them, but I keep pushing them away. The pain is too fresh, raw and aching. So instead of pressing, I reach a hand back over my shoulder and thread my fingers through his hair. It's heated from the last of the sun, the strands silky against my skin.

His hot breath sighs over my neck when he relaxes against me as I let my nails scratch over his scalp. He reminds me of a cat, pushing into my hand, silently asking for more. I turn slowly and look up as he raises his face from my neck. His lids drop as I scratch again lightly. I imagine he'd purr if he could.

"I like that." His voice is like dark honey, rich and sensual. It sends a shiver over my skin.

I can imagine that voice whispering devious things in the night, things that I'm positive I'd beg him to do. For now, I'm content to rise up and kiss him softly before lowering back down. He watches me with his dark eyes, and for just a moment, I see some emotion flicker there. Not love or lust but something dark and ugly.

My heart aches for him. It aches for all of my captains, but Lash, who I admit I first judged harshly, he is maybe the most broken. Stepping back, I let my hand slide down his arm and take his hand, pulling him toward the fire. He lets me, then sits and pulls me down. I settle on his lap, leaning my head against his shoulder.

"Tell me about all of you when you were younger," I ask him, and he tenses for a second before relaxing. "Not about the things that happened but about yourselves."

"We were wild. Hagen was quiet, always a watcher. Sometimes it kept him out of trouble. Fallon was a diplomat; he argued for us, took punishments for us. Cyder was unbreakable, untamable. Before I was taken, I lived on a farm. My family raised horses, caught wild ones to break and sell. Once there was a black one with a long, flowing mane that would not be broken. Cyder was like that colt, untrainable. Wilder's family ran a bank of sorts; he learned his numbers from them. He was a tiny kid, skinny, but he could keep track of cargo like no one else the King had in his crews." He stopped, a small smile on his face.

"And you?" I prod gently.

"I was..." He swallows hard. "I was soft. My mother and father had babied me, cherished me, but it left me unprepared for the ship. My mother had always said I was a beautiful boy as she brushed my hair. Our family kept our hair long; my father told me once it was tradition. But on the ship, there was no need for beautiful, long-haired boys." His voice was filled with emotion by the time he finished. "I learned to dance, to entertain." The last was a whisper that broke my heart.

"I can imagine how cute you must have been." The words feel inadequate for the pain I can feel rolling off him.

A beautiful boy on a ship full of evil men. Unfortunately, I can imagine what his life must have been like.

"Does the King allow women on his ships?" I ask quietly.

He shifts me to his side, stands, and paces away. His back is to me, and his muscles strain and ripple against the smooth fabric of his shirt. His fists clench and unclench as I watch him, waiting for the answer I know is coming.

I hate it when it does.

"No." He spins around, rage and shame stamped across his face.

He strides away into the night. It has grown dark as we sat by the fire, and he is lost among the shadows in seconds. I want to go after him but I also know he wouldn't welcome my attention right now. The horrors he must have faced, even with his brothers trying to protect him.

I add wood to the fire, building up the flames while I wait for him. It burns until it's low and still he hasn't come back, so I add wood once again. Brushing off my hands, I walk across the small space between the fire and the shelter and lift a leaf-covered branch. Lowering myself, I settle on the makeshift bed, making sure to leave him room. The light from the fire makes shadows on the leaf wall, and I watch them dance until I start to drift.

I wake as I feel him slide in beside me. He lays with his side at my back but doesn't touch me. To turn or not, that is the question. It isn't a question at all, really. I start to roll over before I even complete the thought. I curve into him, bringing my leg up over his thighs, and he sighs, shifting to pull me closer after maneuvering his arm under my shoulder.

"I'm sorry," I murmur against his chest.

"No, I'm sorry. I shouldn't have left you alone." His breath whispers over my hair, and I can feel his lips touch it gently. "Sometimes, the memories are too close."

"I shouldn't have pressed." I turn my face up to look at his face and hate the haunted look I see there. He reminds me of a boy I once saw cowering behind his brute of a father. He had no bruises but he was beaten, his spirit broken.

"I don't want you to know any of those things. I don't want you to think less of me. To look at me differently." He studies me. "I'm damaged goods, Reyna. Unworthy. Unclean. I don't expect you to love me like you do the others."

"Your past won't make me think less of you," I promise.

"It's not the past. That's the problem." He looks away. "I'm still that boy, entertaining people. Only now I do it to get things for us. Information, goods, whatever is needed. I'm still just a whore."

I open my mouth but close it, for nothing I can think to say will be enough.

"It's okay, sweetheart." He turns back, and I can see the glimmer of tears in his gorgeous dark eyes.

I can see just the hint of golden flecks in them. I hadn't noticed that before. I don't give myself time to question my decision. Instead, I reach up and cup his cheek with my hand. I pause only a moment before I shift myself over on top of him, moving my body along his. He is frozen, watching me intently. I stop only when my lips are almost touching his. I give him the chance to stop me, but he just watches with a hint of hope in those chocolate eyes. His breath is locked in his lungs, and the intensity I see in his eyes makes mine catch.

Moving that last minuscule distance, I touch my lips to his, gently at first, and then I apply more pressure. I feel the instant his resistance melts away and he kisses me back. It isn't a deep, sensual kiss, instead it is heartbreakingly soft. It says more than any of his words, any of my other captains' words. They want me. They desire me. Lash needs me.

I'm supposed to save the world but right in this moment, I only want to save this man.

I lie back, pulling him over me. Opening for him. He kisses me like he is drowning, and I let him. I let him remove my clothing and explore my body, asking nothing from him. He takes his time, kissing every inch of my skin. My nerve endings come alive as he moves to my breasts, lips and tongue laving the hardened flesh. He is gentle, so gentle it hurts.

The forest is quiet around us, and the moss is soft beneath me. I listen to the sound of his kisses, of his sighs, and of his pleasure. He holds his weight off me, making sure I'm as comfortable as possible.

On and on, he kisses, paying attention to the flatness of my stomach and then the dip at my belly button. Lower he goes, until I feel his breath on my core. He pauses looking up at me before finally leaning closer and flicking out his tongue. That first touch makes my muscles jump and my legs twitch. I ache to drag him closer, but this is about what he needs. I fight to stay still as he drinks his fill. My body grows hotter, wetter, and I can feel my release building until he moves back and rises up.

I hate that I see hesitation on his face and reach up, pulling him over me, positioning him at my entrance. Beckoning him.

He moves gently, slowly until I forget myself. My hips rotate, taking him deep, but still he just rocks slowly into my body. The feeling of it reminds me of the motion on the ships. Just a never-ending swaying into me, over my nerves, and I grow wetter.

My body comes more alive, my desire to show him what love could look like tangling with his need to be loved. My hands run over his shoulder and sides, avoiding the scars, allowing him to avoid the memories. I touch him everywhere I can reach with my hands and my mouth until I raise my head and catch his lips. I kiss him softly, sweetly, as his brokenness tears my heart into pieces, and I hold tightly to him as he falls apart.

Moving my lips to near his ear, I whisper, "Are you okay?"

His movements never change, just a constant onslaught of my body and senses as he focuses on my face. There is something so profound in having his eyes locked on mine as he moves within me.

"How do I explain?" He looks down our bodies and then back into my eyes. "When you touch me, it feels like the first time, like something brand new. Like I'm brand new."

I feel a smile curve my lips as I close the distance between our lips. This time when I kiss him, he kisses me back with a new hunger, and the slow gentle kiss picks up speed as I raise my hips to meet him.

His movements and my emotions send me crashing over the edge, and I cry out, clinging to him. His hands cup my cheeks as he braces on his forearms, and he reaches his release staring into my eyes.

I hold him tightly as we both try to understand what just happened. It was the most beautiful thing I've ever done with another person. I can feel my soul reaching for his. He is mine. Mine to love, mine to protect. No one will hurt him, ever again.

"There will be no more dancing," I murmur against his neck, and his arms tighten around me.

"Only for you." His voice is thick with emotion, and I can feel tears pricking at my eyes. "I will never be worthy of what you have given me."

"Shhh… I won't hear anything like that," I admonish gently while raising my head and looking at him intently.

"Lash." I force him to open his eyes and look at me. I see tears shining in his eyes, just like in my own. "You are worth so much more than what I can give you."

"No. You. This. It's everything." He traces over my cheek with a single finger, and the reverence in that touch is almost my undoing.

I tilt my head, inviting a kiss, and he doesn't let me down. It is gentle and filled with love and so much emotion that I can practically taste it.

"We should get some rest," he says as he breaks away, his lips still touching mine like he can't stand the idea of not kissing me.

"Is it far to wherever we are going?"

"It is quite a distance, but honestly, I'm not sure how long it will take since I've never traveled by land. We will go north through the forest until we hit the coast and from there, we will follow it around."

I nod and then snuggle in closer, my body searching for more warmth. "I'm glad it's summer and not winter."

"It will still be cold at night and along the water," he warns, tightening his arms as he turns us and curves his body around me. "Don't fall asleep before we get dressed."

"You'll have to let me go." I chuckle but hold on tight to him.

His lips feather over my neck and I shiver. "Come on, my queen, let's get you dressed and as warm as we can." He pulls away, and for a moment, I feel the loss of him desperately, which makes me pause.

He hands me my pants and shirt, not noticing. Pulling them on, I ponder the gut-wrenching ache.

Something has shifted in me. I had not felt this with the others. I watch him as he dresses, hating the fabric for covering his golden skin. I wish I had more answers.

"I'm going to add wood to the fire." He stands, pulling up his pants as he does.

I watch him walk away, the thoughts of how I'm changing deep down inside once again bothering me.

"Are you watching? Do you know what's happening to me? Can you give me answers? Can you help me? Help them?" I whisper to the night.

No answers come from the darkness. I wasn't really expecting them to. I don't need confirmation. I can feel the changes happening.

I'm changing. I'm becoming something...more.

CHAPTER EIGHT
LASH

*S*he looked at me with love, touched me with love.

Adding more wood to the fire, I keep my back to her, not wanting her to see my face and the emotions I know are carved into it. I wish she hadn't seen the scars, both outside and in. I know she could feel my shame. She still wanted me. I feel like my dirtiness contaminated her, but maybe instead, she helped clean some of it away. Maybe her touch healed some of the wounds.

I swallow hard. Could her love wash it all away? Could I become new with her?

I'm terrified to hope.

A yip cuts through the air, and I throw some more wood on the fire, sending the flames high into the air.

"Lash," she calls, and I know I've put it off as long as I can.

Joining her, I lay down and pull her near, putting my body between her and any predators that might come close in the night.

"They won't come in unless they are starving," she says calmly. "We always have coyotes around the village but only during the winter do they venture in."

Reyna sounds half asleep already as I pull the grasses and leaves around her.

"I'll keep you safe." The words whisper over her hair.

"Maybe I'll keep you safe." Her words are slightly slurred, and I feel her lips curve against my chest.

'Maybe you already are.' I don't say the words out loud as I stare out into the night.

Hours later and my eyes are growing heavy when I see the glowing gold and red of eyes just outside the light of fire. Not moving, I let my eyes roam over the area around us. Ten or more pairs are watching us, and I tense. Reyna sighs and turns in her sleep, and the eyes shift.

They're not coming closer but growing more interested as a growl sounds from above. I let my eyes roll up, trying to see through the roof she had created, and through a small gap, I can see it silhouetted against the moon. A large wolf sitting on the edge of the cliff, watching those that have surrounded us. It could easily jump down on us, just as the others could easily crash through the sides and drag us out to the pack.

They don't. No one moves except Reyna, who is restless in her sleep.

She startles me when her hand shoots up, fingers outstretched, reaching. Unease skates over my skin as an animal howls then another yips. Wolves and coyotes encircle us.

I've not spent much time on land since I was small but I do know two predators do not work together like this. I ease up, careful not to disturb her. I move to sit in the opening, blocking her from those watching eyes.

"Has he sent you?" I whisper, looking up at what must be the alpha above us.

The great black beast just blinks, its eyes not leaving the woman behind me. I only know he blinks because the gold disappears for a moment. The image of the whale plays through my head as I remember the sea teeming with creatures she called forth. I let my gaze drift around the clearing once again.

"Has she called you to guard us?" It would have seemed crazy days ago, but now I look back at her, her hand has lowered back to her side, and I turn my head back to the fire that has burned low. "I would give my life for her."

A huge white wolf steps from the darkness. It's the yang to the black one's yin. His mate. She draws near, her lips pulled back in a snarl, but she doesn't attack. My hand is on the knife at my side, but somehow I know I won't need it.

"Do you feel her magic? Feel her power?"

The female sits out of range but within striking distance. She is watching not me but the woman sleeping behind me. I don't want to take my eyes from her but I do, once again looking around the edge of the clearing before tipping my gaze up to the massive wolf above us. His head is moving like my own, but he is watching the area around us, watching the forest.

"Protecting us," I whisper and look around again. "Protecting her."

The female whines as she lays down with her muzzle on her front legs, still staring at me. The others in the shadows shift; I only know because I can hear the slight rustle of the undergrowth.

The alpha growls and the hairs on my neck stand up. Danger. Something or someone is in the forest. I reach back and touch Reyna gently. She jerks, sitting up instantly, her hand gripping at my shirt.

"What is it?" She whispers; her voice is steady, and I'm proud of her.

"There are wolves surrounding us but..." I pause as her eyes widen more and they flick from side to side searching.

"But they seem to be protecting us, or at least you. Slow movements though, just in case."

"Protecting us?" She whispers, and her voice is filled with the emotions I'm feeling.

"I think so. I think your magic called them."

"How?" The pitch of her voice has raised a few octaves.

I want to shrug and I'm tempted to ask 'how should I know,' but I don't want to upset her or the wolves, just in case she did call them.

"I don't know, love," I answer, reaching back to pull her closer as she curls herself around my back. "But the alpha just got nervous." I jerk my head up and I can feel her slowly tilt her face up to the sky.

"Holy shit. He's almost as big as Liam."

"Try to get them to do something," I suggest.

Her head whips back down and her face is right next to mine, her eyes staring at me like I'm insane.

"How in the hell would I do that? I don't know how I even got them here, if I did." She sounds incredulous.

"Maybe you just think it," I offer.

She opens her mouth then closes it as the female lunges to her feet and races away. From the sounds coming from the darkness, the others are following her. It only takes seconds before the sounds of the night are all I can hear.

"Did you do that?" I look at her as she shifts around me, squeezing out of the shelter and pushes up to her feet.

She paces away then stops. "I don't think so but how would I know?"

"Maybe try calling them back. If you did it in your sleep, maybe you just need to think it," I suggest.

"Okay. Okay," she mumbles as she turns in a circle, eyes scanning the forest around us. "Okay. Think."

Reyna moves her head from side to side while rolling her shoulders, and I fight a chuckle that is threatening to bubble up. Muscles loosened and brow furrowed, she finally stops and stares out into the night, saying nothing. I take my eyes off her to look out at the forest, also hoping to see some movement.

Nothing.

Minutes later, she spins to look at me. "What good is power if I don't know how to use it?" Her anger makes her face flush a pale pink.

"You will figure it out. We have time." I stand and cross to her, pulling her into my arms as I say the words. "The last time it worked, you were worried about Hagen. Maybe it is tied to your emotions."

The theory sounds right to me, but she seems unconvinced. I press my face into her hair and breathe deeply, smelling us.

Us. I still can't believe she chose me. Me. Out of all my brothers.

CHAPTER NINE
REYNA

I cling to him, squeezing him tight for a minute, letting him feel my emotions before I move back half a step. Looking up into his dark eyes, I see wonder and love.

"What?" He asks when I've stared at his face for at least a minute.

"You love me." I make it a statement but I feel a fluttering as I wait for him to respond.

He swallows once, twice, then a third time. "I don't know. You chose me."

"Chose you?" I smile to soften the question.

"I was first. That means something, right?" I hate the doubt that has crept into his voice.

"Yes." I think of how I should explain. "I don't know if this is going to sound right." I stop, unsure if I should even say anything more.

"Just say it," he urges, but I can see the hint of fear shining at me from his eyes.

"The others want me and I want them. I even need them. I need all of you. But you need me back…" I trail off, pulling my lower lip between my teeth and chewing at it.

He reaches up and runs his thumb over that lip, freeing it from the torture of my teeth.

"I do and I don't mind that's the reason. I just want it to become more."

I smile, letting my breath rush out. "Just give me a little time to love you like you should be loved and soon you won't question why you were first. Can I tell you something?"

He nods, his thumb still sliding over my lower lip, his eyes focused on it now.

"Each of you mean or represent something different to me. I think, for me anyway, it is how it will all work. How we will be a family."

His thumb stops and he looks back up into my eyes. "Family. Yes, we are your family."

My heart breaks for my mother and father, but they are gone and I must survive this world I've been thrust into. I must protect these men when I hadn't been able to protect my family and friends. Friends. I have been so focused on my family I had barely thought of the people I had grown up with—of Margo who had gone against the other girls to be my friend, of Charles who kissed me sweetly behind the pub when we were both twelve.

My home was in flames when Fallon pulled me away into the darkness. I don't know who, if any, are left alive.

"Hey, where are you?" Lash's voice is near my ear.

"Sorry, I was thinking of home. Do you think we could go there when this is all over?" I halfway want him to say no, for I'm afraid there will be no one left.

"Of course. But for now, I think we should try to get some sleep before we start at first light. I haven't heard anything but the wolves, and as far as I can tell, they are trying to keep at least you safe."

I let him lead me back to the shelter. I didn't expect to fall asleep, but it didn't take long for his warmth to relax my muscles and sleep came soon after.

A twig snaps and my eyes fly open. I know the sound before I am even fully awake. His hand grips my hand and I look up at him. His finger is raised to his lips, a wicked blade resting against his cheek as he watches me to make sure I understand. I nod once and he rolls slowly, as if in sleep, but I know his eyes are searching just like my own. My face is at the curve of his neck, and I peer into the trees barely lit by the lightening of the sky. The fire had died, and only a wisp of smoke floating up hints that there had been one at all.

"I smelled the smoke," a delicate voice calls out just before a petite woman with long ebony hair steps into the open.

"Where did you come from?" Lash replies as he sits the blade held loosely in his hand. Before she can answer, he pushes up with his other hand to stand.

She holds her hands out, palms up, before taking another step into the clearing.

"That's close enough," Lash sounds menacing, and for some reason, it surprises me.

I shift to my knees and crawl completely ungracefully from the shelter. Standing, I put my hand on his forearm.

"These are dangerous times, so forgive us if we are a bit untrusting," I offer with a small smile but I watch our guest closely. "We were just about to leave."

"Very dangerous for some," she says and Lash stiffens. "But the danger is not from me. I saw the ships. They saw your skiff."

"Fuck." Lash spins looking toward the coast.

"They saw it floating." She grins. "They are searching along the shore."

"You untied it." She nods at my statement. "Why?"

She shrugs. "If I saw the smoke, they will too." She points

86

across from us. "That small peak there in the distance—walk toward it but keep it just on your left. If you do, you will find the northern coast."

"What if we had planned to go south?" Lash's eyes are narrow as he glares at her.

"Your friends went north. Follow the peak and you just might get in front of them, if you move quickly." She turns and steps back into the trees. "Good luck."

She disappears silently, which suggests that she let us hear her before.

"Let's go." I grab his hand and start to pull him the direction she had given us.

"We're just going to trust her?" He asks incredulously.

"Last night, I asked him for help." I don't have to say who. "I think he may have been listening."

* * *

SHE CROSSES into the other realm as soon as she walks into the trees, out of sight and time. Pausing, she looks back at them, wondering if she should tell any of the others. Nestor has nudged here and there, but she has always stayed out of it.

But this time, she felt the magic, had heard the prayer.

Old power is awakening.

CHAPTER TEN
LASH

I don't trust the woman.

Although that in itself doesn't mean much, since I trust no one other than my brothers and now Reyna. Reyna. I can't really say I trust her; I don't distrust her. I'm giving her my heart or at least, I'm trying to. I want to. I don't trust her with my back though, not yet.

Maybe never.

Even with my brothers, only Wilder has my total trust. It's stupid but that's how trauma works, or so I've been told by Wilder, who devoured every book he could find in the city libraries about abuse of every kind. It's his role in our family—he tries to fix us, to make us better. He is the one to be at our side when the nightmares come and our demons are punishing us once again.

Sometimes we hide it. I hide it more than the others, locking myself away and keeping separate from everyone. My crew takes over when I have my darkest days, or nights, as it most often is, and usually after a trip to the shore. I do my job, but it is always at a price.

My brothers have offered to let me stop, but it is what I'm

good at. I can smile and flirt while dying on the inside. I can let them touch my body while locking myself away. I am the spy. I become someone else and I learn their secrets.

"Lash." Reyna's voice sounds far away as the darkness threatens to break free, I blink and throw another lock on the black door in my mind.

"Sorry. I don't trust her."

"Why would she lie? Does the King have women on his crews?" I shake my head at her question. "She came from the forest."

She's not wrong, but still, I look at the area where she faded away into the trees.

"I will follow you. I trust you." Reyna locks eyes with me, and I feel something settle.

Trust is such a strange and powerful emotion.

I sigh, weighing our options—follow the path the women suggested and possibly catch up with the ships or go with my original plan and hope we catch them at the safe haven. She just stands, waiting for me to make my decision. Complete faith. Complete trust.

"Let's head toward the peak." I move to the stream and splash water onto the smoldering fire while Reyna breaks apart the shelter scattering the pieces. In minutes, there is barely a trace of us that remains. "I think they could miss this if they aren't looking too closely."

She nods and holds out her hand. I take it. We have nothing but the bag that is slung over my shoulder. In it is what little food we have left from our picnic. It's not enough to get us to my brothers, unless we intercept them. I have one knife to protect us from the men searching for us on the shore.

I hope she's right and whoever she prayed to is listening.

We walk in silence for an extremely long time. I keep glancing at her at my side. She is looking around at the forest, and I wonder if she is avoiding looking at me. But just as my anxiety pushed me to my breaking point, her fingers wrap around mine.

My nerves settle.

"You know I had very few friends growing up." Reyna keeps looking at the trees. "I was different from everyone else in my village. Of course, my parents told me how I had been left for them. They told me how much they loved me, how I had been a gift, but it didn't change the fact that I looked different. I acted different. It didn't change that the other kids, and, hell, even some of the adults, were vicious to me."

She looks at me, and I squeeze her hand.

"Don't get me wrong, I had a good life and my parents loved me so much. There are a few times that, well, I don't want to go into details. It was bad, that's all you really need to know. Nothing like your childhood, but moments were bad." She lets her voice trail off.

"Sometimes the kids are much worse than the adults," I murmur.

"Most times. I wish it had been the same for you." She stops walking and turns to me. "You don't have to hide how you feel from me."

"I shut people out. I hide myself away." It's the only explanation I can give.

"That's okay. Hide away until you feel safe," she whispers, a small, sad smile curving her lips. "I haven't shown you all of myself. We all keep parts of ourselves hidden. We protect ourselves, and you and my other captains have more reasons than anyone, so protect yourself. I will be here when you need me. And some day, we will protect each other."

She turns away, starting to walk away and just leaving me to stand there and watch her go. Could she be perfect?

I think about how she was with the others—funny, brave,

studious, and unsure. Now with me, she is vulnerable. She is the perfect blend of all of us.

Created for us? Or were we created for her?

If I believe she is to become a queen or something even more to save the world, it isn't so hard to believe we would all fit perfectly.

"Why did they let it all happen to us?" I don't try to hide the anger.

She stops and looks back at me, where I'm still frozen.

"I don't know. I read a book once that asked why the God that created the world let bad things happen." I raise my eyebrows, waiting for her to tell me what she'd found. "Sorry, no real answers, but it was basically that there was a reason for everything."

I huff. "Bullshit."

"I know, but maybe they can only affect fate or destiny in certain ways. Maybe destiny is linked to our lives, each small event a guiding point on our trip to where we are meant to be." She shrugs then holds out her hand.

"There are more things in heaven and earth, Horatio." I repeat the words from the story Wilder had read to me while we lived in the great library in our city.

"What's that from? I like it."

"Wilder read so many stories to us while we lived in the city. That was from Hamlet, by a man called Shakespeare," I tell her. I don't know why I even remember it.

"I hate that so much was lost—so many stories, so much history." She pulls at my hand as soon as I grip her fingers. "Come on. You can tell me stories while we walk."

"Stories about what?"

"I don't care. About your brothers, about yourself, or just stories that Wilder read to you." She looks at me with nothing short of puppy dog eyes. "It will pass the time," she says after I don't respond for a minute.

I think, letting my memories flow through my mind like leaves caught on a breeze. I imagine myself plucking one from the wind, praying it's a good one. I choose a story of the time when we first reached the city that time forgot.

We were still kids, starved and basically dying.

"We went wild when we found ourselves crawling into the empty city. We had seen ruins before, but this was just pristine. It was clean and perfect. We found pictures later that showed the city, just as it was. Actually, that isn't true, it is cleaner, brighter." I smile at the image in my head. "I found this little glass thing. It had a scene in it, and when you shook it, snow fell. I feel like New Orleans is the same, without the snow. Like an invisible glass dome protected it."

"Maybe he has… Or they have. Maybe the city was or is important to them." She looks up at me and I realize I hadn't even noticed she had drifted back to my side. "It could be important to us. It already was to you and the others."

"Yes, it was."

Her pointing it out makes me think about fate or The Fates. Everything that I read, after Wilder taught us all to read, about them said they were known to be vindictive bitches.

The war was said to be between ancient gods, and it seems like maybe there was a war going on right now and we just didn't know about it.

"Do you think this one guy, god, whatever, is the only one left?" I ask but I already have my own idea of the answer.

"I don't know, because the letter said the others had withdrawn. The winners had left us to our fate," she murmurs with a small frown on her face.

Interesting that she uses that word. Fate.

I don't like it. I don't like the idea of someone pulling my strings, our strings.

I want to talk to my brothers. I want to turn around and

track the King and rip Cyder from his hands. Instead, I start toward her, following her once again since I had slowed in my anger.

We walk in silence, hours ticking by, and I can tell her brain is whirling. Mine is doing the same. Plotting their deaths.

"We are like game pieces, aren't we?" She finally says, just as the sun is beginning to set.

We've travelled miles. She walks fast, especially once she begins to get angry. She stops and spins around, glaring at me.

"I'm beginning to believe so." I don't like how resigned my voice sounds. "I want to talk to my brothers."

Did that sound whiny? I think it did. Her smile confirms my thought; it's indulgent.

"I understand. I want Liam." Her eyes focus on the way we had travelled throughout the day, and there is worry clouding the Caribbean color of her eyes. "Do you think he's safe?"

I want to say yes but I can't be sure and I won't lie to her.

"I don't know but I can't imagine hardly anything that could get the best of that hound. He took down a moose on his own. You get that isn't normal, right?" I study her face, hoping to see a hint of relief.

Her eyes drift back to my face and there it is. "He is very different. Special. I remember the day I found him, or rather, he found me. I was reading in the woods in my hiding spot. He burst through a bush much like he still does now. At first, I thought he was something coming to eat me, but he just stood looking at me."

"Did you ever see any others like him?" I ask but I know the answer.

"No." Her eyes drift again. "He has been my best friend since that moment."

"What did your parents think?"

"My dad was sure he was an adult when I brought him home, but then he kept growing. People were scared of him at first and remained wary, but he never hurt anyone. He is just my friend." Her eyes are shining when she looks back at me once again.

"Your protector," I assert. "He's protecting you, even now."

"I guess. I just wish he was here."

"He will find you," I promise.

"I hope you're right." She doesn't sound convinced.

"If he doesn't find you, I will find him." This time, I reach out and take her face in my hands and force her to see the truth in my eyes.

"Thank you," she whispers and finally she lets a tear fall.

"You don't have to be strong with me, Reyna. Your life has been blown up and you are allowed to be sad. You are allowed to be anything you want. Get pissed. Hit something. Hit me. Let this power that is forming in you free." I get close to her. My breath puffs over her face, her hair moving with it, but I want her to listen.

"I'm not going to hit you. I would never hit you," she says, her arms closing around me tightly. "Never."

"You can't keep all of your emotions locked away. It's not good for you." My lips move against her ebony hair. "I've done that and at some point, you either explode or implode," I try to warn her.

She doesn't pry, and I think I love her for it. I can't talk about what I did. I don't know if I will ever be able to.

"Come on, we should keep moving." I straighten some, and she slowly releases me and steps away but she keeps her hand on me.

Taking that hand in mine, I squeeze it, trying to tell her how I feel, my heart pounding so hard I'm positive she can hear it. She squeezes back and that pounding slows, settling to a smooth steady rhythm.

Reyna lets me lead her away with one last look behind us.

'You better be okay, you freaking beast.' I send the thought out into the universe. *'If you are watching us, directing all this, if you are listening, you better bring that hound back to her or I WILL find you.'*

It might not be wise to threaten some enormously powerful being, but I couldn't care less if he or they come for me.

I would welcome death on my best days.

CHAPTER ELEVEN
CYDER

*D*eath would be a blessing.

I have been back in his hands for mere hours, and yet it is like I've never left. I'm not the captain of a ship; I am not the man I've fought so hard to become; I am once again the starving, broken child, terrified of the sound of a whip in the air.

My skin is untouched, but with every small noise, I flinch. I'm in the hull, in the room. Our room. It is unchanged, except it now holds the meager things of other boys.

It smells the same, like fear and sweat. Blood. Tears. Vomit. All of the things that I've tried to forget... They flood through my mind. I can feel my muscles quivering. I know I'm not alone. I cast my gaze around as much as I can without turning my head. I search the shadows, my breath coming faster than I want.

I do not want to give him my fear.

I will give him not one more part of myself.

A slight scraping of fabric against something causes my body to tense, and I clench my teeth, bracing for pain. None comes but instead cool, soft fingers tickle over my scars, and I grind my teeth even harder.

It isn't the King who stands so close behind me.

The fingers trace the criss-cross pattern before stopping in between my shoulder blades. There the scars are the worst, red and raised, puckered, and the skin is tight from the many layers.

I shiver when a nail scratches over the area.

"They are quite lovely," a feminine voice whispers, and I can feel breath on the same scars.

"Fuck you," I growl.

Bell-like laughter echoes in the darkness.

"Oh, my dear, while I would certainly enjoy myself, I have something much more enjoyable for me," the voice whispers close again. "I'm going to let you pay a tiny part of his debt."

I don't want to ask, but as the silence stretches and my back grows warm under her hand, I can't seem to stop myself.

"Whose debt?" I hate that my voice shakes.

"Nestor, the great Egyptian god. The one that has deemed you worthy. Worthy but not enough to save you from all this." Her fingers trace the scars again. "And now, you will have more because he will not save you this time either."

"I don't need to be saved." I let my rage bolster my courage.

More laughter greets my ears and it sounds like pure evil. A cold sweat breaks out over my body. I am going to die in this room.

"If you kill me, how will this Nestor person know?" I ask.

"I'm not going to kill you, and we aren't staying in this disgusting room."

That surprises me. "The King will not let me go."

"He can't stop me. He wouldn't try." Her breath is against my neck. "He knows better."

The last words carry a deadly threat.

I find the information curious and file it away, in case I survive whatever she has planned for me. We are game pieces on a board, and these two beings are moving us around. The knowledge ignites a fire within me. It isn't a new idea but for some reason, in this very moment, it solidifies an anger that has been smoldering in me since the moment my mother was killed in front of me.

Over the years, I have tried to extinguish the fire, but it is always there burning.

"We should go." The fingers snap by my ears and the chains that have been cutting into my wrists holding my hands stretched above my head disappear.

Completely disappear. My arms drop and instantly my nerves scream in pain as the blood begins to flow back into them. Still, I don't turn around. She drags her fingers over my skin, moving around me. I roll my eyes up, not wanting to see her. I'm still looking at the dark ceiling when I feel my body shifting.

Shifting from the room and through space, maybe time. I've felt nothing like it. Magic. Power. It is wondrous and frightening.

The darkness fades to bright blue sky.

Lowering my eyes, I look around and see we are now standing on the edge of a tall cliff, the sea crashing below on jagged rocks.

"Where are we?" I ask, still not looking at her.

"Look." She points. I can see her hand in my peripheral and follow the direction with my gaze.

I can see ships tiny in the distance. Five tiny ships. My brothers.

"Brothers," I scream like a warrior going into battle and as the word dies away, I realize this is part of my torture.

When I finally force my eyes to turn down and look at the

woman in front of me, my breath catches. She is literally breathtaking. Otherworldly. Definitely something other than human.

Alabaster porcelain skin with midnight hair that hangs down to her waist. She smiles and it highlights the whiteness of her perfectly straight teeth and ruby red lips. Lips not stained by makeup but naturally bright red. Dark lashes frame eyes the color of an opal. I had seen some in a store in New Orleans. They are truly unnatural looking. Captivating. I find I can't look away.

Trapped.

She is a spider and I'm caught in her web.

"Nestor. I know you are searching. Listening. Watching," she whispers, but I feel magic in the words. "Come save your chosen."

I'm frozen. Muscles locked into place.

"Do you know who I am?" She asks, her hand still on my chest. "Speak."

I'm released from some of the bonds she has locked around me. Just enough to do as she commanded.

"No." I want to add 'you crazy bitch' but I refrain.

I have my role in our group. I watch people, studying them. I find their tells, their weaknesses, and if I remain quiet, I will start to learn hers. I can tell already she lets her emotions drive her.

Gods are much more human than they would like to think.

Powerful but weak, just like we are weak.

This goddess is letting anger drive her. What would anger a goddess so much that she would stay to get her revenge when all others have left us in the hell they created?

Love.

I narrow my eyes, watching. Waiting.

Tell me your secrets.

"I am Nemesis." She pauses looking at my face.

I keep my face blank and instead look her up and down. She is wearing her clothes like armor—black leather pants, black-lace up boots up to her knees, a wide-brimmed black hat currently held in one hand, and a shirt made from black raven feathers. When she held out her arm, it had looked like a wing. It has hints of blue when the sun shines on it, like it is right now.

"The Goddess," she says and her voice has grown harder.

"Sorry. With the apocalypse and all, we didn't really have a chance to read up on ancient gods," I quip, poking the hornets' nest a little.

I can hear her teeth grit.

"You should always take the time to learn about your betters." She smiles but it is laced with poison. "We were meant to rule you and be worshipped." Her voice softens as I feel the scrape of nails over the skin just at the base of my throat. "Would you like to worship me?"

"Pass." I smile back and put as much disgust as I can into it while hiding the fear that is making my muscles twitch.

"Don't you want to know how I was worshipped?" Her beautiful face is a mask of innocence.

"Not really." I really, really don't because while my first thought was sex, now I fear something altogether worse.

"I am the Goddess of Revenge, of retribution... I require blood and bone. I like death as a gift most." She is practically singing to herself, and I wonder what horrible memory she is reliving. "I'm afraid you, Cyder, will offer a tribute. You are the sacrificial lamb to lure Nestor from his hiding place."

The nail is suddenly longer and much sharper. I hold steady as I feel the sting of the first cut and the warmth of my blood running down my chest.

Her eyes are practically glowing with excitement at my reaction, or lack thereof.

"I don't know this Nestor that you think will come for me." I keep my voice level.

"Sure, you do; you just don't know it." Another cut. "I taught a man once. He wanted to know how to draw out his revenge, how to savor that which he had longed for many years. I showed him the art of a thousand cuts."

Nemesis rips my shirt from my frozen body and once again smiles, and I notice that her teeth all have tiny sharp points.

'Were they like that a moment ago?' I ask myself.

No. Just like her nails weren't talons before but they are now.

'You just don't know it.' Her words play through my mind. I search my mind for faces or a face that appears again and again, but it's out of place. I see him. I've seen him on every ship. He has been in different towns, his appearance slightly different, but it's the same man.

"Now you know." She is watching me closely. "Was he on the King's ship?"

I flinch at the question because while I don't have a memory of it, I'm sure she wouldn't ask if she wasn't sure that he had been.

"He let them do this to you." Her claw cuts one of the scars on my back.

Shivers crawl over my skin as I feel the warm roughness of her tongue. Cat-like.

"Pain makes the blood taste so much sweeter," she purrs, and I think it is more to herself than to me.

"So what did this person do to you?" I ask as I feel another small slice.

I'm sure at some point I will stop feeling each cut. I can't help the picture that crashes into my mind. Her power is holding me up, and I know I will stay like this until she lets my dead body drop. I test my arms, but they stay frozen, held out from my body. I think of the images in the church I had often visited in the city. Jesus on the cross. Crucified. I am almost in the same position, and the fact is not lost on me.

I will die for another's sins.

"Is Jesus the son of God?" I ask, thinking about the stories I had read about the man.

"A god." She smirks.

I don't know what answer I thought I'd get, but that wasn't it. Another cut.

"So this Nestor did what exactly? I figure if I'm going to die for him, I should at least know why," I ask again.

"He did many things. He sided with the humans. He killed our people. He killed God... My love. They killed my brother. And now, he is meddling." She looks out at the water, not even paying attention as she cuts my skin again.

"With my brothers and me?" I don't mention anyone else.

"And the woman." She steps around me, locking eyes with me and letting me see a hint of anger. "Oh yes, I know you found her. My spy told me what she did with the sea creatures. I know the power is calling to her. I also know I won't let her get it."

"You would give it to a sadistic killer?" I can't hide my revulsion, I don't even try to.

"Maybe," she evades.

She plans to get it for herself.

"Why don't you just go take it? If it is takeable." I watch for those micro reactions people just can't hide, no matter how hard they try.

Muscles tighten around her eyes, and the vein in her neck and along her temple pulses. So human-like. She moves so fast that my eyes can't track, and this time, the cut is deeper across my chest. More blood. This time, I see her arm flash back, arcing over her head.

Maybe not a thousand cuts, then. Good.

My only regret is not being able to warn the others. I let my eyes fall closed, and my head drops forward. Surrender. The feeling tastes foreign on my tongue. Never once have I given in, not to him, not to any of the others that thought I was fair game or that my brothers were. I have more than whip scars on my body. It is foreign but somehow I feel calm. Not relaxed, but like a soul deep calmness.

'If you are listening, don't come. I'm not worth it. Save the others. Save her. If you are as powerful as I think you are, protect them. Do you know Nemesis is here? You aren't the only one playing this game.'

"I wanted to make this last but maybe I will just leave you for him to find." Her breath moves the strands of hair that have come free from the braids along the top of my head. "Goodbye, Cyder. I had hoped you were like the Celts of old but I guess not."

I feel outrage flood my system and I jerk my head up hard, cracking her in the face. I understand the mistake as soon as I see her blood smile.

"It could have been quick but now..." She licks at the blood on her lips, and I watch as it coats her wicked teeth.

I brace for pain.

A low growl makes the hair on my neck rise, and I turn my head as her eyes narrow on something to our left, just within the shadows of the trees.

I feel my own eyes widen.

Red eyes shine in the darkness, almost level with my own. What beast is this?

"It's not possible." Her voice has a hint of fear in it.

What would scare a goddess?

A moment later, I know as the creature steps from the trees. It looks like Reyna's beast but not exactly. It's bigger for one, twice the size of Liam, and the skin isn't covered with his rough brown fur. Instead it is black, but more. It is more like the complete absence of color.

"Hellhound," she whispers and starts to back away. "Where is your master? Where is Cerberus? Where is Hades?" Her eyes dart left and right.

I don't know who those people are but if they scare her, I can just imagine. I think about the stories in the book about the ancient ones. Cerberus was a giant three-headed dog that guarded the Underworld.

This beast has one head that it has lowered to look at her. Another growl vibrates the air.

"You aren't supposed to be here," she whispers, but I see that she is shifting positions, preparing to fight.

A howl echoes from somewhere near, but the animal never takes its eyes from her.

"I think you are about to be outnumbered," I murmur softly, unwilling to draw the animal's attention.

"I guess I should go then." She smiles and it is the one filled with poison. Pure evil.

I don't have time to question what it means before she splits me open and disappears. As soon as she's gone, I fall. My hands coming to clutch my stomach, to hold my guts in.

Fuck. I blink as tears fill my eyes. I lay there, staring up at the sky that reminds me of the water I love so much. A rustle alerts me to the animal's approach, and I turn my head, locking eyes with it.

"You tried." I forgive the animal who creeps closer.

Another howl and this time, it does look away and then back at me. I swear I can see a sadness that matches my own. The hound keeps coming and then crouches down, the great black nose sniffing at the wound, and I don't know why but I reach out, laying my hand on the dark fur. It is the softest thing I've ever touched but also the hottest. I know my hand will be blistered, but it doesn't matter.

I'm dead anyway.

The animal flinches but then pushes its body against my hand just as darkness takes me. My last thoughts are of peace and love.

Weird.

CHAPTER TWELVE
REYNA

I swear I hear Liam. I swear he is close but in front of us somehow.

I glance over at Lash; his brows are furrowed and his eyes are darting from side to side.

"It's Liam, I know it," I tell him.

"I believe you, but how did he get in front? Although, maybe it's just a trick from the hills and mountains. An echo, maybe." He turns, looking behind us.

"Maybe." I say it but feel that isn't it.

Another howl cuts the silence that has surrounded us. That isn't Liam. It is unnatural, making my skin crawl, and I fight my need to run. It's the inherent fear prey has of a predator.

"Fuck. What was that?" Lash spins again, moving in closer to my side, protective.

"Something that kills."

It is a statement. I know it in my bones. I search the shadows cast by the trees around us, flinching as another howl, even closer, cuts through the forest. This one isn't the same as the others.

"That was the alpha from the pack that has been watching us," Lash whispers as he leans close. "We need to move."

I'm frozen.

"Now!" He pulls at me, dragging me a little to get me moving.

"Lash, what if something is hunting Liam?" My heart pounds at the thought of anything happening to him.

"I'm more worried that something is hunting us." He pulls more then looks down at me, and whatever he sees makes his face soften. "I'm sure Liam can take care of himself."

"But..." I start but stop, unwilling to put voice to my dark thoughts.

"Let's just get someplace not so vulnerable," he urges, and I start to follow him as he turns away.

He doesn't run but we are walking as fast as possible, his head turning side to side. Searching. Protecting.

I'm gasping when he finally stops. The peak the woman had pointed out looms huge in front of us. We still have a long walk tomorrow to reach the coast but we've come much farther than I thought we'd get. The almost-running helped us cover a bunch of ground.

"There." He points to a small crevice in the stone.

I wonder if it is like the place I had hidden Fallon. The image of the mysterious woman pops into my head. Could it have been the man? Can he be any shape? Any person? Any animal?

"Could the one directing all this be anything? You know, any person or thing?" I murmur, and he whips his head around to look down at me.

I can tell the thought really disturbs him. Sadness washes through me. The differences in our lives are only highlighted by our reactions. I thought the idea to be exciting; he seemed to feel instant distrust. I hate it. I hate that they have all gone through so much. I hate the scars that have been left.

"I don't know. What are you thinking?" His eyes scan the area around us.

"I just... I don't know... wondered at what he might be capable of doing. The crevice looks a little like the one that was in the cave I hid Fallon in." I look toward the narrow opening once again.

"You think he sent us here?"

"I don't know what to think. All of this is insane. I just wondered." I sigh before stepping toward the opening. "I don't really know anything about the war or the people who fought in it. The gods." I peer into the opening and see just enough room for the two of us, but it would be a tight fit. "Not like the cave. Maybe my imagination is getting the better of me."

"I doubt it. I don't know if anyone really remembers the gods. From what I understand from the books we've found, they were thought to be myths, just stories from a time long before the war. What they are capable of is anyone's guess." Lash looks over my head into the small cave. "Cozy."

I grin as he waggles his eyebrows and I feel a flutter low in my stomach. Before I can second guess myself, I rise up and kiss him, lingering over his full lower lip.

My breath catches as he deepens the kiss. Letting my arms slide around him, I press against him. A deep rumbling moan fills my mouth, and I drink in his desire.

Rustling in the trees near us tears us apart, and he pushes me into the tiny cave, blocking the entrance with his body. I once again appreciate the wideness of his shoulders and the way his waist is tapered in. My eyes lock on the curve of his ass just as I hear him clear his throat. I look up to see him staring at me, but his fake stern look can't hide the heat in his eyes.

"We are being stalked, and you're staring at my ass."

"I couldn't see anything else since you shoved me in here

so I figured why not enjoy the view I had? Did you see anything?" I lean to one side, trying to look around him.

"It's the wolves, but they are nervous. The female is pacing just there." He steps back and points to the trees we had just left.

I see her as she moves between two tall, wide pines. Her ears keep swiveling and her head is low. She watches us, only stopping her movement when a huge black male moves to her side. I push out around Lash. Time to test this power.

"Come to me," I murmur as my eyes focus on the female.

She takes a step but the male nips at her shoulder, stopping her, protecting her. It is he that comes, answering the call of my magic.

MY magic. My brain stumbles over the thought.

"Reyna," Lash warns as the wolf comes ever closer.

I can feel many eyes on us as the alpha draws near. His lips curl back in a snarl, but he doesn't try to hurt me. I kneel, ignoring Lash's angry whisper about being reckless and stupid.

"I won't hurt you," I tell the animal, who is now within my reach. "I know you won't hurt me. Thank you for watching over us." I hold my hand out slightly but stop when he growls. "Sorry." I let my hand drop as my eyes focus on the female and now another large male moving close to protect their alpha. "Is there something else in the woods?" I ask and then I try to think it.

Nothing happens. I don't know what I thought would.

"Anything?" Lash asks, meaning it, believing in me.

I reach back and touch his leg. "No. I don't even know if I'm doing it right. Or if that is part of these mysterious powers. But thank you."

His hand closes over mine and he squeezes gently. "I have faith in you, not the magic we think you might wield."

My heart pounds at the significance of his words. Maybe

more than sweet words of love or even trust, it's faith that I can help them. Faith that I can help save them. Saving the world is obviously important, but them believing I can save the family we want to create, when I couldn't save my own family, is... I don't even have a word to describe the feeling.

His faith. It pushes me to try again. I reach for them, picturing my thoughts, my question flowing to them. The alpha locks golden eyes on mine, and I feel it before I see it. Just a tingle of awareness, of sentience, knowledge, and then the image hits me like a ton of bricks.

My breath lodges in my lungs. Terror. There is no other word for the feeling that is coursing through me, that has frozen my muscles in place. Terror.

A beast. It can be described no other way. Towering over any animal I've ever seen, in person or in books. It is black, the absence of light, except for the red of its eyes. Snowy white fangs were revealed as the lips were pulled back in a snarl. I could feel the fear as it rolled off the alpha and the other wolves in the pack.

I turn my head as if in slow motion and look at Lash, and he reacts immediately to my face and the emotions racing over it.

"Monster," I stutter over the word and he nods, turning his back to watch behind us.

I look back at the pack. *'Where?'*

The female spins and paces away toward the coast. Her mate yips at her, stopping her, and she snarls. I get another impression but I don't understand it. Frowning, I send my thanks, and they spin away, disappearing into the trees.

Lash waits for me, not pushing for more information while I try to get my fear under control.

Finally, I swallow and turn to him. "Something is in the forest, near the water. Something unnatural and not of this earth. It is a creature that makes Liam look like a tiny pup. I just got the impression of somewhere near the water."

He tenses at the description. "They are fucking with us again. Aren't they?"

"I don't know if the one who is directing us is or if it's that someone else is working against us. Could the creature belong to the King?" I ask but I'm almost positive of the answer he's going to give me.

"No." His head shakes. "He has never had any kind of beast. Can you describe it any better?"

"Not really. I just got their impressions and felt their fear." I frown, trying to pull more information for him, but there just isn't anything else. Just fear from the whole pack, which scares me more than the image.

They hunt together, can take down huge prey, and this thing had sent them running. It's still in the forest and it could be looking for us right now. The thought chills me.

"What if it follows them to us?"

He purses his lips, and I realize that he had already thought of that, which was why he had been watching the trees around us.

"Should we move?" I glance around.

"I think we should be fine here. They will let us know if it comes close." He moves away and starts to clean an area outside the small opening. "I'll get a fire if you find some wood."

I start to move away from the granite face of the imposing cliff face, but his voice stops me.

"Stay close though."

Normally I'd bristle at an order but I know it is said out of care and worry so I just nod before moving into the tree-line. There is plenty of dry wood, so I load up my arms while keeping an eye on Lash and the darkness around me. I pause as a thought creeps into my mind. Darkness… The thing that the wolves saw was exactly that—darkness. I shift my eyes over every patch of darkness, searching for any hint of red. I don't breathe until I finish and begin to hustle back to Lash's side, dropping the wood in my arms. I stay at his side as he moves around the area picking up large stones. He says nothing but hands a few to me as he grabs the last two from the ground. I follow him back to the cleared area and hand the stones to him after he places the others he had in his hands around the bare ground.

"You okay?" He finally asks as he strikes a rock against another making a spark.

I hadn't even seen him tuck the wad of dry grass in the middle of the circle. Smoke drifts up then a small flame appears as he snaps twigs from the pile of wood I had dropped.

"I just spooked myself," I admit.

"I'll keep you safe." A promise… But is it one he can keep?

I don't doubt his sincerity, but this creature, it could kill us both.

"Come sit down. We don't have food but we can get warm. The fire will keep most animals away and with the rocks at our backs, we should be safe until morning."

I look around at the quickly darkening sky as I lower myself down. "Maybe in the morning, we can find some berries or some kind of food." On cue, my stomach rumbles.

We sit watching the flames as the moon rises.

Exhaustion forces us into the alcove and into a restless sleep. He lays in front of me, blocking the opening. Protecting me in every way he can.

I wake. No, something wakes me. Blinking, I try to focus on what had disturbed me. Silence greets me, only broken by the sound of Lash's deep breaths.

Unease crawls through me.

Something woke me.

I reach out with the power that has also been awoken.

CHAPTER THIRTEEN

"*B*urn it all."

I listen to him bark orders. The King that I made, the King that seems to be forgetting that fact.

"Burn them, along with their homes," he calls out, and I stiffen, looking out at the villagers huddled together.

Children are clinging to their mothers, and I lock eyes with a young man, his arms around a young woman. Anger and hatred makes his shine like diamonds. I focus on how the girl is holding him. Not lovers, no. I held my brother just like she's holding hers.

I've hung onto Hypnos the same way. I was holding onto him just like that when Nestor murdered him.

"Leave the people."

He straightens from his slightly slumped position at my words.

"I'm the King here," he growls, and I think it's time to remind him of who I am.

I hit him with a hint of my power and drive him to his knees. Exactly where humans should be when in front of me.

"I made you a king. You will do well to remember where I

found you." To remind him, I rip the memories from where he has buried them, using my magic to make them real for him.

I smile as I watch the terrified boy manifest right before my eyes, tears filling his eyes. Locking them away, I bend down and smile when he focuses on me. I swallow the anguish that is wafting from his body, drinking it down like ambrosia.

"Leave them," I order. "Or those memories will be nothing in comparison to what I will do to you."

I sift to half a dimension away, where I can see him and make sure he does what he was told.

I grin again when he calls out and his voice shakes. "Get on the ships."

Moving to his side, I whisper to him, "She is already with the boys you so carelessly threw away. Stop searching the villages. You shouldn't have lost them."

"You took him. You took our key to finding them," he growls.

I drive him down with my power once again, rage coursing through me, as I see the beast coming at me on the cliff top.

How had it gotten here? Who had sent it?

Nestor?

I hate not knowing who all is playing this game. Those traitors locked the power away, gave up what was ours and then left after killing so many. The biggest traitor was Nestor, but then again, he had betrayed me a thousand years before the war had even begun.

The cries of those around us drag me from the memories, and I realize my power has washed out from me and is punishing all of the pirates and quite a few of those from the village.

I am known for my ability to exact revenge or help a

person get their revenge, but retribution, that is my true talent. I use their own guilt, no matter how tiny it might be, no matter how they have buried it. My power pulls it out and forces them to relive their transgressions.

I feed on their emotions, gulping down the guilt.

Moments later, I pull my power back and let myself move through the dimensions to my home. I haven't been here in a hundred years, unwilling to face the emptiness. It looks just like it did on the last day of the war.

My family hadn't joined the fight and for that, they had been killed. Slaughtered.

Nestor had once been welcome, but that was when the humans had still been struggling in their caves. We had been so young, so innocent.

He killed that innocence.

My palace needs an update in preparation for my new rule. I start removing things that are too painful to look at. Other items—things of my mother's, a bow that had been my brother's—I keep. I trail my fingers over the intricate carvings along the riser. I remember when he carved it.

Shaking my head, I scatter the memories. Instead, I focus on the present and try to figure out how to best direct the players in this game.

"Fuck," I scream, angry once again that I can't claim the power myself. "It will destroy you," I remind myself.

I must stay the course. The girl is the key. I have set the plan in motion and I have to trust that I have made the right choice.

The King will capture her and break her, and then she will be mine to control, along with the power held within her.

I will use her to destroy Nestor and those he helped. Humans. Humans in our world. A disgusting betrayal. We came to this world to escape our own and then we were forced behind the veil by the creatures that we had helped.

I hate him.

I have been alone for so long. The others that survived the war have hidden themselves away even here. I haven't seen them as I've travelled throughout our world, other than those that sided with the humans. I've stayed far from them. My temper is well known, and I don't try to keep it under control.

Why would I? I am a goddess.

CHAPTER FOURTEEN
FALLON

*T*he seas are rough, with waves battering the ships as we turn out of the channel.

"Lower the mainsail," I call out, and my men rush to get it lowered, slowing the ship so I can watch as my brothers pull through the narrow opening.

The channel is more like a funnel, and in the final one hundred yards, the ships have mere inches between the rock cliffs and the sides. I hold my breath as Wilder's ship eases out and I can see the Lust come into view. The crew works under the direction of the first mate but they are somber without their captain.

They do the same as I and lower their sail, gliding up alongside of us. Grabbing the swing rope that is hanging down at my side and running back and then forward, I fling myself over to them.

"He will be working his way with Reyna to the rendezvous point," I assure them when they all pause to look my way. "Our biggest concern is Cyder."

My anger and fear surge at my own words, and on cue, Cyder's ship comes into view. The crew is tense as they come through the narrow opening and drop the sail. Silence envelopes the ship, no chatter or banter, just angry silence.

A crew without their captain. Us without our brother.

I watch it slide in beside us as the other ships come through the opening. Hagen's is last and it drops its anchor, swinging its starboard side around. The gun ports rise and cannons slide out.

Hagen wastes no time.

Cyder's crew straightens as the guns fire and rocks crash into the water.

The channel is no more.

The King can't follow us, but now neither can Cyder, if he breaks free.

I haven't let go of the rope and as I pull it tight in my hand, I nod at the first mate. "Trap it."

He nods, and there is a flurry of movement as I cross back to my own ship. A shrill whistle cuts through the air, and four ships begin to move. Cyder's first mate drops the anchor, and I hear him call the crew to the deck.

He knows what I know, what my brothers know. Someone betrayed Cyder. Someone betrayed us. Another reckoning is at hand.

It's clear that Travis isn't the traitor, for he is waiting with knives held loosely in his hands and death in his eyes when I swing across to Cyder's ship. Moments later, Wilder and Hagen join me. Hagen's face is dark with rage, but Wilder's calmness is lethal.

I watch as he steps forward, his sword held down against his leg but drawn already. Some of the crew shifts slightly, and we take note of who. Hagen glances at me as we wait for Wilder. Our brother doesn't get angry often but when he does, he is a force to be reckoned with.

"Bring us the betrayer." The demand was whispered, one

that can't be ignored. "Bring him to us or suffer my wrath. Your honor has been destroyed."

Hagen and I don't move from our positions at his back. The silence is only broken by random throat clearing. We don't speak as Travis moves through his men, eyes searching, reading their faces.

Travis moves to stand between his crew mates and us, drawing up to his full height, and once again stares at them.

"The captain would give up his life for any of us, and someone has betrayed not just him, but also us. Someone led them to us. Someone let them on our ship. Someone gave Captain to them. Someone has handed him over for torture..." he stumbles over his next words. "Or death."

We are still silent as a young man I haven't noticed before steps forward. Tears are in his eyes.

"They have my sister." He swallows. "It's no excuse, but I had to try to save her."

No one moves, except to turn their heads toward us.

"Jamie?" Travis' face says it all. Disbelief.

"They caught us three years ago. Maggie was just eight, and he kept us after he did horrible things to our momma. He gave me one option, get on one of your ships or she will be..." The boy starts to sob.

I watch as Wilder's body relaxes, but at the same time, his body is rigid with outrage. I reach out and lay my hand on his shoulder, and he steps back.

"Travis." The man turns his head to look at me. "Bring him to my ship." I turn to leave them, knowing he will do as I ordered.

I can hear Wilder and Hagen moving right behind me. We don't stop until we are in my quarters.

"Cyder would not want him killed, but something must be done. We must find all of his spies." Hagen paces while rubbing his hand over his short hair.

"How do we do it though?" Wilder flops into the chair by the table.

"No idea." Hagen punches the thick beam that runs the length of the ship.

"First thing we have to do is question the boy," I murmur while thinking out loud. "He has to be communicating with them somehow."

On cue, there is a knock at the door. Hagen stops pacing and Wilder sits up straighter as I turn to the door and call out.

"Enter." My voice is hard.

They enter, the boy first, his head held up and back straight. Travis closes the door silently behind them. Jamie walks to the chair that Hagen slams down in front of him then sits.

"I deserve any punishment. I only ask that you try to save her," he asks, his voice steady.

"We make no promises," Hagen growls and the boy nods, his fists clenching in his lap.

"How did you get Cyder to bring you onboard?" I watch him as I speak.

"That was my fault, sir," Travis declares from near the door, ready to face any consequence.

"Don't punish him, please. The King learned you would take in certain types of boys and he placed me in a place I would be found. I played my part and did what I was told." Jamie's voice didn't waver.

I glance at my brothers, gauging their moods. Anger, but I also sense sympathy for the position the boy was put in. What wouldn't we do for each other? Nothing.

"Does he know all of our ports?" Again, I watch for those tiny expressions people can't hide.

"No, only that you have gotten supplies at certain places before." No deception on his face.

121

"Where is your sister?" Wilder asks, and only Hagen and I can hear the heartache in his voice.

We weren't all only children when we were stolen away.

"His ship. There is a small room with marks all over the walls."

I cringe, knowing exactly what room he's speaking of. Hagen visibly flinches, knowing who made those marks, and Wilder looks away, hiding his reaction. She was locked in our room. No, not a room. Our cell.

Prison.

Hell.

"Fuck." Hagen punches the beam again.

"He's never kept a girl," Wilder says, his voice low. "The crew."

He doesn't continue; he doesn't need to. They are animals. An eleven-year-old girl doesn't stand a chance of surviving them.

"He gave me two years, and I only had a few months left to give him one of you." The boy has tears in his eyes.

"Are there more on the ships?" Hagen strides to the young man, his steps pounding over the worn wood of my floor as he stops inches from the boy.

"Yes." He moves and Hagen stiffens but the boy just pushes his sleeve up and shows us a small eye tattoo on the inside of his elbow. "He marked all of us to remind us he was watching."

Hagen straightens and strides out. I trust him to go through every crew including my own.

"Travis, go back to your ship. Leave Jamie here. I will handle him from now on." Travis nods and I can see he feels for the young man but will never trust him on his ship again. "Jamie, follow me."

The boy nods and stands, ready for his punishment.

Wilder stays in the chair, and I leave him to get his thoughts together before he heads back to his own ship.

Climbing down the ladder, I lead the boy down into the belly of my ship, straight to the galley and to Kellihan. I trust the man to watch the boy, and he happens to have one of the few places that can be locked on the ship.

"Kellihan?" I call out as I step into the kitchen.

"Captain." The older man calls from a dark corner, and I turn at the sound.

"This is Jamie, the one that gave them Cyder." Kellihan pushes up, fire in his eyes. He has long thought of us as his own. "King has his sister locked in our old...room." I choke out the word.

"A girl." Two words that speak volumes.

"Yes." I turn to look at Jamie slouched behind me. His arms are wrapped around his midsection and tighten at Kellihan's tone. "Jamie, one more question."

He nods, his face turning up to look at me.

"Are there more in that room?"

He blinks slowly and his face falls more. "I...I never even..." He trails off.

"That's okay, boy." Kellihan comes around the side of the huge butcher block island and stands at Jamie's side. "What do you want me to do with him?"

He watches me closely, waiting. "Put him in the larder." I look at Jamie and then the man I consider a father. "It is for his own safety as much as punishment." Kellihan smiles slightly and nods, and I don't miss the hint of pride in his eyes.

I turn and leave him to it, rushing through the ship to the deck. My door is open, and I know Wilder has gone to search his own ship. Jack is waiting for me.

"Gather the crew. Get four men you trust completely and

have them bring each person, one at a time, to me in my quarters," I order as I stride through my door.

I close my door behind me and lean against it. Glancing at the wall, I have an urge to follow Hagen's example but I'll keep my knuckles intact, in case I need to kill someone soon.

Next my eyes turn to Reyna's chest sitting in the corner, and I push off the door, crossing to it. We had all looked at the paintings but we hadn't studied them. Lifting it up, I place the dark wood on my desk and sit, running my fingers over each of the latches releasing the hidden locks. The lid opens soundlessly, and I look inside as I begin to hear movement outside my door. Instead of going for the final picture, I lift the letter and pull out the first painting. The women in it are breathtaking, and the men at their sides are formidable.

Otherworldly. Magical.

Tearing my eyes from the people, I focus on the scene around them. When Reyna had pulled it from the chest and showed it to us, it had felt familiar to me somehow. Just a niggling thought at the back of my mind. I stare and stare, focusing on every tiny detail, but my frustration grows as I just can't grab hold of the thread. A knock at my door saves me from myself. Placing the painting back inside, along with the letter, I close the lid and place the chest on the floor behind me.

"Enter," I call, and Jack opens the door stepping inside.

"Everyone is gathered, Captain."

"Send in the first person."

Jack looks back and jerks his hand.

We go through the crew one at a time. No one even blinks when they are told to strip and their body is searched.

Each one hears the same thing as they leave. "Keep your mouths shut." Each one nods, just a jerk of acknowledgement.

The door opens as the current crew member leaves and the next comes in. I know as soon as I see him.

"Strip." He glares, and I simply wait as Jack repeats the word. "Strip. Or I will do it for you." He flips a nasty looking blade in his hand.

The man stands defiant.

"I know the eye is on you. Show us." I lean back in my chair as I lock eyes with the man.

I don't know his name or how long he's been on my ship.

"When did he join us?" My eyes stay on him.

"Just before your accident," Jack growls, his eyes are hard.

"So the man we killed wasn't working alone." I steeple my fingers in front of me.

The man is still standing stiff and defiant in front of me. "Jack."

My first mate opens the door and jerks his head. Two men file in the door shutting behind them.

"Hold him," I command as I rise.

The man fights as they grab him, and I hold out my hand. Jack places his knife in my palm as I stop in front of the King's man. He struggles more as I reach out and grab his shirt. My blade nicks his chest, causing blood to seep from the small cut. Then the knife cuts through the coarse fabric in my hand like it's nothing. I slice from top to bottom then let Jack pull the remnants from the man's body. There on the inside of one of his outstretched arms is the eye.

This is no boy that is being coerced. This man came here to hurt us, to destroy us, and I feel no remorse in my next action.

The blade cuts through his neck the same as it did the fabric, and he stops fighting. He stands in silence until his legs buckle then the men drag him out.

"Bring in the next, Jack," I say as I wipe off his blade on my sleeve then hand it back to him.

He turns, stepping over the pool of blood to pull the door open wider, and motions with his hand. The next man enters and stops just outside the edge of the blood, his eyes focusing on me.

"Strip." Jack's voice is like a whip, but the man doesn't flinch.

This goes on for the next hour. Two more traitors are found, and I kill them without remorse. Kellihan comes in last, and I shake my head as he begins to pull off his shirt.

"No one needs to see your wrinkly old ass, Kelli," I grouse at him.

Jack barks out a laugh when the old man shoves his pants down. "Jesus, Kellihan." He shakes his head as the man bends over, flashing said wrinkly ass at us both as he jerks his pants up.

"How many?" I hate the tiredness I hear in his voice.

"Three in total, here. I haven't heard from the others yet." I run my fingers through my hair.

"I'm gonna go make you something to eat," he mumbles.

I don't argue, for I learned years ago not to, as it does no good. He glances at me, assessing me, and I fight to school my face.

"Jack, go bother the crew," he growls. "And find someone to clean up this blood."

Jack winks at me as he leaves. We all do as Kellihan says.

The door closes quietly, and while I have no doubt that he will do as asked, I also know that he will give us some time.

"Kelli," I say, waiting for him to say whatever is on his mind.

He rubs over the hair on his chin, and I know he won't be rushed. He steps around the blood and then crosses to the chair, sitting gingerly. I am reminded of his age, although I'd never say that to him.

"I love you boys as if you're my own," he starts, and there

126

is a waver in his voice that makes me swallow hard. "I should have saved you all and now…"

"Kellihan, this is not your fault," I argue, and he holds up his hand, the knuckles swollen and arthritic.

"I should have killed him the first day I stepped on his ship. I knew he was evil down in the core of him. But I looked away and I continued to look away." He looks up at me, and for the first time, I see tears in his eyes.

I swallow again and clench my teeth.

"I let you down and I let myself down. Don't let this war turn you into something you're not." His eyes flick to the blood then focus on me again. "Let her keep you whole, and I hope you can forgive an old man his weakness."

"Nothing to forgive." I barely manage to get the words out, and faster than I imagined he could, he is up and out the door.

'Let her keep you whole.'

His words break something loose inside me. Both infinite sadness and bottomless rage roll within me. I haven't been whole for years. We were broken apart the moment the King came into our lives. It's not fair to expect Reyna to fix us, but I can't help but wish for that very thing.

I wish.

Shaking my head, I push up from my chair and try to shove my feelings back down, because wishing is stupid. Turning the doorknob, I jerk the door open and almost run into the kid standing there with a mop and bucket.

I bite back a harsh comment as he falls back a step, trying to get out of my way, fear stamped upon his face.

Swallowing, I tighten my hold on my emotions. "Sorry. Go ahead and go in." I nod and try to soften the look on my face, but he still looks down and steps around me.

Another damaged boy we picked up along the way. He's better but like us, he will always be fighting the demons and darkness. I didn't help any just now but I will deal with it later. Now I have to focus on the pit of vipers in our midst. Walking to the rail, I grab the swing rope and cross to Wilder's ship. He is slumped on the long chair in his quarters.

"How many?" I ask as I lean against the doorjamb, arms crossed over my chest.

"Four. Have you checked the other ships?" He doesn't look up.

"No. I had three." I push off the wall and walk across to him, sitting at his side. "Travis is checking his crew now." He nods, still looking down. "Wilder, it will get better." I'm trying to convince myself as much as I am him.

"When?" He mumbles, looking up.

"I don't know, but it will."

"I hope you're right."

So do I. So do I. "Are you going to be okay?"

Wilder locks eyes with me, and I watch as he tries to shake the morose feelings off. "Yes. Let's go check on Lash's crew." He nods then stands.

I follow his lead then follow him out the door.

Night has fallen, but I can see the stain of blood on his deck in the pale light of the moon. The Howling Lust is anchored to the left and near the bow of the ship. It is quiet, no sounds of laughter or the crew talking amongst themselves.

Holden, Lash's first mate, is waiting for us. He looks solemn as we approach him.

"How many?" I ask as soon as we draw near.

"None, sir." Pride radiates from him.

"None?" Wilder asks, as surprised as I am.

"I checked them all myself, Captain, from top to bottom, and no one had the eye on them."

"Good, Holden. That's very good." I glance around and

see men standing in the shadows watching. "You're all worried about Lash."

He nods, his eyes moving over the crew. "We don't like leaving him behind. He…" He trails off when a man clears his throat from the left somewhere.

"He what?" I straighten and glance in the mystery man's direction.

I'm not surprised when the man steps from where he has been leaning. He is a beast of a man that I've seen many times but I don't know his name.

"Dylan," Wilder supplies by way of greeting.

"He needs us," Dylan says and his deep voice is hard.

"Needs you?" I question again. "For?" Weakness can be taken advantage of and I won't let that happen to Lash ever again.

"We keep our Captain safe. We keep his demons at bay and allow him the space he needs." His eyes are hard, and I can hear the accusation in his voice.

"Wilder?" I turn to look at my brother at my side.

"It is Lash's story to tell, not mine and not yours." He looks at Dylan and the others hard. "I'm very glad there were no traitors here." Spinning away, he leaves me standing here confused.

"Holden." I nod once and leave them, following Wilder to Hagen's ship which is next to us. "We will discuss this," I warn Wilder.

"Like I said, it is Lash's story. I won't tell it."

I blink at the hardness of not only his face but also his voice. Wilder is our gentle soul, or voice of reason.

"I'm just concerned," I murmur and feel horrible at the instant remorse that shows on his face.

"I know but I can't tell you his secrets."

Secrets. They wrap around us and bind us as tightly as

any chains. We all have them, but I've often worried about Lash. Fuck, I've worried about them all.

I was there first.

I was there when they were all dragged in, crying and frightened, and thrown into that dark hole. It was me that held my hand over their mouths to silence their cries, to try and save them from that first beating. Hagen was first, no hand needed for the angry golden-haired boy with fire in his eyes. The same fire that is blazing in them now as he looks across the water at us.

His hand is wrapped around a swing rope which he whips over to us, and my own hand flicks out to grab it without me even thinking to do it. Stepping up to the railing, I throw myself across, harder than I need to, but my anger and frustration get the better of me.

Hagen raises a brow as I land hard on his dark deck. I just shake my head as I toss the rope back to Wilder. Hagen just stares at me.

"It's just been a shit day, Hagen," I mumble, rubbing my hand over my face.

"Oh I know that for sure. I had two on my ship," he growls.

"Two isn't bad. I had more." I frown.

"Luckily, they had just joined the crew the last time we picked up fuel." He hits the rail, and I notice the blood on his knuckles.

"Do we know how they were communicating?" Wilder asks as his boots hit the rail. He stands there balancing, his eyes focused somewhere on the horizon.

Hagen shakes his head. "No, but they must have been. How else would they have found us in the channel? As far as I can tell from talking to people, no one even knew it was there."

"Are you sure they didn't just follow us in?"

"Fallon, you know better than that," Hagen admonishes.

"I know but I just... I want this over. I want all of this fucking shit over." Even I can hear the tiredness and defeat in my voice and I hate it.

"Brother." Hagen steps near and his fingers close over my forearm, tightening for a moment before releasing me.

It's as close to a hug as I will get from him. I've wondered about his life before the ship, but he's never spoken of it. Wilder exchanges a look with me, and I know he thinks like I do. Hagen's life was shit before he was locked in the belly of the King's ship. Hagen didn't cry, ever. He has more scars than the rest of us because he wouldn't give them the satisfaction of crying out.

He was forged in fire.

"I will kill them all for what they are trying to take from me. From us." Where my voice sounded tired, his sounds elated at the thought. "My sails will be painted red from their blood."

I look up as the wind shifts and blows through the wolf head standard that Hagen has mounted on a long pole by his helm. The long tail attached whips from side to side, and the eerie shrill whine from the wolf's head cuts through the silence of the night.

Hagen is like the Dacian warriors he had fashioned the standard after. It's funny how we all found a small part of ourselves in the legends of ancient warrior tribes. Although I don't know that I am like any of them, Hagen is most definitely like the stories of the Dacian warriors, the legends of vampires and werewolves born of the bloody destruction left in their wake.

"I know you will." And I do, for I have no doubt he will kill as many of the pirates chasing us as he can. "We will get Cyder back."

"And Lash and Reyna." His tone and his face brook no argument.

"Of course, but they, as far as we know, are not being held by a mad man."

"The key words are 'as far as we know,'" Hagen argues.

I know him well enough to know there will be no arguing with him so I don't respond again.

Finally, he looks over at me. "Sorry. I hate that they were here, on my home."

"We all do, brother," Wilder whispers as he reaches out to pat Hagen on the shoulder, but the gesture isn't well received, and Hagen jerks out from under the comfort that is being offered.

Wilder just lets his hand drop as he jerks his head at me, and I nod. We will leave him to his anger.

"We are going to go check with Travis. I will let you know what I find out there and then I will go ask Jaime how he let them know where we were." He jerks his head once but doesn't take his eyes off the horizon. "We will leave in the morning. It might give Lash and Reyna time to catch up to us."

A grunted noncommittal response is all I get but it is enough.

Following Wilder's lead, I leave him to his anger. We all cope—or don't, depending on how you look at it—in different ways. Travis is waiting for us by the rail when we swing to the middle of our ships. We still have the Rising Dragon trapped between us. His face is solemn but his eyes hold fire and determination.

"How many more, Travis?" Wilder is looking at the other members of the crew that are gathered on the deck.

"Two. They have been here a few months less than Jamie. They have been dealt with."

"Hooah," the men on deck yell as they hit their chest with their fist. The thumps are loud in the quiet of the night.

Travis lets them continue for a few moments, their voices growing louder, and then I turn as I hear other crews joining in.

A battle cry.

"Good," I call as their voices begin to die down. "We will question Jamie and then decide how to proceed. Did any of the others have similar stories of loved ones being held?"

"No, Captain. They were just bastards looking to get the King what he wanted. Just fuckers who wanted to hurt us," Travis growls, and I watch as his fists clench and unclench repeatedly.

Blood stains his skin, and I know those he ferreted out had died hard. Good.

"We leave at dawn. Get your ship in order." I turn to leave, but voices stop me.

"Our captain."

"We won't leave without our captain."

Many other outcries are uttered, all with the same meaning. They are willing to die to get Cyder back.

"We will but we have to figure out how. Lash knows to rendezvous at Green Cove and he has Reyna with him. Her newfound talents might help us find your captain," I remind them of the woman who is supposed to help save us all.

I hear more grumbles, but Travis turns and glares at all of them. "You think they don't want to save Cyder, then you need to leave this ship. These men are brothers, a bond forged in hell. They would not leave him behind. Our captain would not let you question them, and nor will I. Get back to your stations. Now!" He barks the last when no one moves.

They all start to shuffle away, still not happy with the idea of leaving their captain behind.

I nod at Travis and then swing back to my own ship. I assume Wilder will do the same.

Exhaustion hits me like a wave washing through me. It's that type of tired that goes bone deep. Pushing open my door, I look down at the floor. It is spotless, as if it had never been coated in blood. It smells like orange blossoms and some other scent that I don't know the name of but reminds me of dark, humid nights. A candle flickers on the table, and I know it's probably from Kellihan. He cooks up more than food in the kitchen.

As I draw near, the secondary scent becomes stronger and I know the boy had cleaned the floor with a cleaner containing orange oil. It too was probably sent by Kellihan.

I skip the couch and throw myself across the bed.

The monsters come as soon as darkness drags me under.

CHAPTER FIFTEEN
CYDER

I am lost.

Dead. The pain is gone, all except the echoes of it that my mind won't let go of. It's dark, not like night but like the depths of the sea. My body is floating. I can't tell if I'm up or down. Wilder has told us of heaven and hell, but I'm not sure I'm in either.

I've read all the books on myths and magic. Those books often talked of other realms, other worlds where creatures dwell. I wonder if I am there. I wonder if I am just delirious with fever, lying on the ground.

Although, if that were the case, I should hear birds or wind in the trees, something, but there is nothing. It is silent.

Completely.

Just like the darkness, it is not just silent but the absence of sound.

It is like the trunk he would lock me in, but worse. He being my father. Our life with the King was horrible, but my life was terrible before. At first, when the pirates came and killed my family, I sighed with relief, even through my tears. The tears were for my mother and my sister. The sigh was because the monster was dead and could no longer hurt us. At the time, I didn't know there were other monsters in the world. I was just happy I'd never be back in the trunk, locked away for hours or sometimes a few days. Not long enough to kill me, just long enough for my pleas to stop. I hadn't learned that pleading with a monster does nothing but give them pleasure.

He hadn't started hurting Maggie. She looked just like him, whereas I looked like my mom. I spent hours wondering if he had ever loved her. I know now he didn't; he just wished to possess her. Break her. He used me and then my sister to bind her to him.

Colleen MacAskill was a proud wild woman with hair like a sunset and eyes the color of clover. Her skin was like mine, pale even when we had been in the sun, except for the freckles that formed constellations on her cheeks. Often those freckles were hidden by bruises. I remember the softness of her lips as they would brush against my temple; I remember them often rough with dried blood. But she never broke. She fought him and the pirates until she drew her last breath.

My brothers have often talked about how the memories, the faces of their parents, are fading, how they remember less and less of their life, but I still remember. I remember both my monster and the angel that tried to save me.

My father is the reason the King could never break me.

Memories of torture filter through my mind, and I wonder if this is purgatory. I had read about it in one of Wilder's books. A place to repent for sins. I have many. I always thought that if heaven and hell were real, I would go straight to hell. I've done horrible things in order to survive, to protect those I consider family.

Maybe this is hell, my own personal trunk, and I'm locked in with all my memories.

I feel flames licking at me. Hell it is, then. I smile but it's more like a grimace. I'm burning. Either I'm dead and in the flames of hell or I'm dying and the heat is from a raging fever.

I think it's the flames. I've had a fever, had one that almost killed me after I refused to give the King what he wanted and he whipped me until my bones were bare. He then threw me in a dark room, thinking the isolation would break me when the lashes didn't. He didn't know I had been shaped in the darkness. The fever had all but killed me, but Kellihan saved me, convincing the King I was worth more alive. I hated him for that for a very long time.

This feels different.

At least my death kept me from telling the King anything about Reyna or her possible powers. I kept my honor. I just wish I could have warned them about the 'Goddess.' The monstrous dog was a surprise. A blessing.

I saw intelligence. Knowledge.

My muscles jump and my heart pounds as a scream shatters the silence.

I am not alone.

Turning my eyes, I search the darkness, straining my ears for any sound. Nothing. Seconds tick by, turning into minutes and then longer. How long, I don't know exactly, but I am once again wrapped in silence.

I remain alert and flinch when I hear nails on stone or glass. The beast or another creature all together. My ego says fight, but my body knows I cannot. The clicking draws near, then I feel the subtle graze of fur.

"Where am I?" I ask, and my words are swallowed, falling silent before they are even free of my mouth.

Not dead. Not on earth. Where?

I'm still trying to figure it out when I feel myself falling.

Falling back to earth? Falling up? Falling down?

I don't know but in moments, I feel grass beneath my burning flesh. Blinking, I try to focus on my surroundings. The beast is all I can see and I fight a scream as it once agains licks at my wounds.

I fail. Birds take flight and the insects fall quiet at the sound that is ripped from my throat. A howl drowns out my voice. Closing my mouth, I listen to the mournfulness of the sound. It is both terrifying and sad.

My eyes have fallen closed, for the pain is too great, and I fear I will be jerked back into the darkness.

The beast howls again and this time, I hear something far away respond to its call. The licking stops, and I crack my eyes as the breath that had been caught in my lungs explodes from my throat. The great dog or wolf or hellhound, whatever it is, has lifted its massive head and is looking south of us.

I don't think it was expecting something to answer it.

Its head turns back to me, and bright red eyes lock onto my own.

"Friend of yours?" Its head turns much like any other dog as it listens to my stupid question. "No, I don't think so. Are you a friend or foe? Friend, it seems." I draw a breath but keep it shallow, since I feel like I've been gutted, which I have. My mind is racing as a name pops into it. "Do you know Nestor?"

That got her attention.

"So you do. Did he send you?" Of course, the beast doesn't answer. I must be delusional for even asking. "You can't tell me, can you? I'm losing my mind."

She lays down at my side, the heat from her burning fur soaks into my muscles, allowing them to relax a miniscule amount.

"Thank you. If he sent you to help, please go find Reyna and Lash. I don't think I'm going to make it, and you're wasting your time here. Save them and leave me to the darkness." I reach out slowly, and she allows me to touch the softness of her muzzle.

Her lip pulls back, and I can see the canine that is curved there is longer than my finger.

"Where are you from?"

She only whines until we both hear the howl from before, but it is much closer. I try to sit up and barely contain the scream that boils up from my burning guts. I smell my burnt flesh, and the scream is replaced with vomit. Turning to my side, I throw up, missing the beast, but she leaps to her feet growling.

Not at me but the forest around us, and I tense. She has been guarding me and now this creature is worried. What could scare something like her?

"Is your master near? If so, now would be a great time to call him."

She growls, but it's a strange sound, low and filled with power. Power that even I can feel. Power like I felt when Reyna was in the water trying to save Hagen. She is calling someone or something for help.

What could this creature call for help? My breath is coming in quick gasps. Shifting, I use my hand to push against part of the wound. She had split me wide open, sternum to below my waistline. And now it's closed but it's nothing but burnt, blistered flesh. Just touching it is enough to make me grind my molars to dust, but I do it to hold it as I try to push myself into a seated position.

I don't want to meet my death on my back.

Something is coming. Someone is coming.

Sweat is pouring down my face and my shirt is stuck to my body when she rubs against my back, supporting me. Holding me upright.

"Thank you." I hadn't even seen her move. I'm having a hard time seeing anything right now as darkness flickers.

"She likes you." A soft voice startles me, and I jerk.

The action causes me to cry out, and I hate it because of the weakness it shows.

"Kyon, how did you get here?" She calls out as she starts across the clearing, moving around us to stand at the cliffs' edge, her back to us.

I watch her, trying to memorize the details of her. Her raven hair that is hanging down to her waist. Two braids run down each side of her face, and beads decorate them. Her waist is slim. She is petite, a tiny woman no taller than a young boy. Her hips are curvy, and even in my current condition, I can appreciate her beauty as she glances back at me and the animal at my back.

"Her name is Kyon?" I say, but my voice is hoarse with pain.

"Yes. Do you know how she got here?" She narrows her eyes before turning her body around.

"No. She saved me, I think. A goddess gutted me but she left when Kyon showed up," I answer her truthfully.

"A goddess." I don't miss the tightening just around her eyes.

"You don't seem surprised by that word."

"Oh, I am, believe me. There haven't been any gods or goddesses here in a very long time." She seems angry, but there are other emotions underneath that anger. "But then, there also haven't been any hellhounds on this plane in even longer."

"Hellhound." I knew it.

"Kyon, I must ask again, who brought you here?" She ignores me and focuses on the beast who shifts, and I hold my weight, letting her know she can move away.

Kyon stands looming over us both and moves in front of

the woman, lowering her head. Neither move or make a sound for long minutes, until finally the woman nods and steps away.

"It seems my Nestor isn't the only one that wishes to help. Kyon came to help one she loves a great deal but she felt the power of the one who did this to you. I must take her back. She could do more harm than good." The woman looks at the charred flesh of my chest and stomach. "No matter her intention."

I just stare at them both. She has admitted to so much.

"Why doesn't your man just help us?" I can't hide my anger, my outrage.

"We can't. We shouldn't. He has done too much already. The power is not ours."

"Who are you?" I wonder if she will give me her name.

"Mimi," she answers without hesitation.

"Can you tell me anything that can help us? Can you get me home?"

She turns back to the sea, and I hold my breath. It puffs out when she and Kyon disappear. Here one second and gone the next, but she has left me here.

Left me to die, most likely, because even though the wound is closed, I can feel my temperature rising. Infection is spreading already. My energy is suddenly depleted, and I fall back, hitting the ground hard.

Fuck. The word sounds slow and slurred in my head as darkness jerks me back.

* * *

I STAND in the middle of hell. Kyon sits at my feet only because I have a magical leash on the hellhound.

"Emma? Jason?" I call before starting forward. "Hello?"

I'm not even sure if the couple is here. I haven't seen

anyone but Nestor for years and years. The others had pulled away from the destruction they had left in the world. I didn't blame them but I had been alive for a very long time and understood that there would always be destruction. In fact, another great battle that could destroy the world was coming.

I sigh as I look around and feel some anger starting to simmer, because it wasn't that destruction was coming. It was already happening. It had been happening for years. It had been quiet, and then Nestor and I had felt a shiver of power in the world. Their kind of power.

Cyder hadn't been wrong in his assessment of my lack of surprise when he mentioned a goddess. I had known another of our kind was roaming the human realm unchecked. I was angry at the others that had chosen to ignore the world they had saved and I was angry at myself for choosing to ignore the threat she knew the hint of power was. Whoever it is, they had tried to hide their power, which means the hint that they felt was just a small amount of what the person had.

A goddess.

It could be any number of their kind.

Kyon whined, pulling at the leash and jerking both my arm and my mind back to the present.

The beautiful redhead that ruled this kingdom with Jason was walking toward me and smiling.

"Mimi, it has been too long. Kyon?"

I hear the frown in the hounds name. "Emma. I didn't think you guys knew she was up topside, wreaking a little havoc."

"No, I did not." Emma looked at Kyon. "Why did you leave?"

I release the magic holding the hound in place and watch as the beast runs to Emma's side. Emma stared into the red eyes for a very long time, and I understood that unlike the impressions I had gleaned from Kyon, Emma was actually talking to the beast.

When she is done, the woman looks shaken but she schools her face, looking at me after a moment.

"Apparently, Jason's sweet girl has been going up to check on the pup that Nestor talked us out of. I didn't realize he wasn't with you guys." Emma studies me.

"He is not. Nestor got him for Remy's last descendent." I don't try to lie because I knew that telling her about the girl would soften any feelings she might have about the hound being loose in the world.

"Remy's..." Just the name, but the flux of power that pulses from her tells me she still cares for the man a great deal. All of the human women that had found magic with the Guardians and our kind loved the man that had painted their futures.

I wish I could tell her he was still alive. I wish I could tell Cora the most, but Nestor and I had agreed that they all needed time to heal from the losses they suffered and to find themselves with their new powers.

Bringing Kyon home and Emma figuring out that Liam had been given to the girl was as close as I can come to breaking my promise to him.

"I don't suppose you want to tell me what's going on." Emma's words force me to focus on her in front of me, not the Emma from hundreds of years ago.

She is truly a queen now.

"I think it's best if I go and you stay here, like you have been," I say without the judgement I often feel.

She sighs, glancing around, and I know who she is looking for but I don't sense him near.

"You would tell me, tell us, if something was happening, wouldn't you?"

I think about her question. Would I? Obviously not,

because something very big is happening, and I won't tell her. If I did, she would tell the others, and they would want to 'help.' We can't take the chance of anything being changed.

The butterfly effect is real. We are all interconnected, and every decision we make could change fate.

"You know how fickle fate is, Emma. You learned all about the strings that join us. You need to trust me. Trust Nestor. We have been watching the world since the war."

She frowns. "We abandoned them. We abandoned you. I'm sorry." She threads her fingers through the burning fur of the hound at her side.

"We understood. But I need you to keep this to yourself." I turn my eyes up. "You know if you tell them, they will come. You know everything will happen as it should. Gaia hasn't abandoned her children."

Emma nods. "If you want this…" she waves her hand at Kyon and then up where my eyes had just been, "all to be a secret, you better get going. Jason knows when anyone enters the Underworld. He will be on his way here even as we speak."

"I'm sorry to put you in this position," I apologize.

"Well, we put you in an even worse position, I fear." Emma turns and walks away, but Kyon doesn't follow.

"I will check on him. Both of them, I promise," I whisper, and she woofs then spins away, leaving me in the dark chamber alone.

Shifting out of the Underworld, I let myself be pulled back to the earth and the chaos that is waiting for me. The tree is still as it was last I visited—growing, with limbs spreading wide.

I greet the tree of life with reverence. "I hope we are doing the right thing." I lay my hand on the trunk and like every time since the war, I receive no response, no hint of the being that used to greet me with love.

CHAPTER SIXTEEN
LASH

*S*he is bathed in pale light.

No. That's not right. She isn't bathed; the light is coming from Reyna. It's beautiful in a way I can't even describe. Pushing up, I move as quietly as I can so I don't disturb her. I don't know what she's doing but I don't think I should bother her.

I frown, realizing that she managed to get over me and out of the small cave without waking me. I shouldn't have fucking slept. I had promised to keep her safe and I failed her.

Her head tilts to one side as if she's listening to something. I strain but I don't hear a thing. The realization makes me frown. I don't hear a single thing. Silence in the forest is not a good thing.

A predator is near.

"Reyna," I call out softly. "Reyna. We need to go."

I climb to my feet and step next to her. She is still gone from this clearing. Her body is practically humming with her new power.

"Reyna, sweetheart, something is coming and we need to go. Now."

She sucks in a harsh breath, her eyes finally focusing on me as her face turns slowly toward me. Her lashes flutter as she blinks repeatedly.

"Lash?" Confusion mars her face as she looks around, noticing the growing light. "Is it morning?"

"Close. We need to go, Reyna. Something is coming."

"It's not coming for us. It is calling us." As if to confirm her statement, a howl unlike any I've ever heard obliterates the silence that we have been wrapped in. "We need to hurry."

She is adamant and before I can say a word, she takes off running.

"Reyna!" I yell, hoping to stop her even as I chase after her. Luckily, the fire had died in the darkness.

Damn, she is fast. I'm gaining on her just when she slides to a halt, her head whipping from side to side. Searching. For what, I have no idea since I don't know what she was hearing or feeling.

"It's just gone. Disappeared." She is still looking, but her feet start moving.

Watching her, I realize she doesn't even know she's moving. Instead, she is gone again, her power pulling her from this world as the search continues for whatever had called so strongly to her.

I follow just behind her as silently as I can, allowing her power to guide her. I just hope that it is actually her power and nothing else pulling us to some unknown fate. I heard the stories, the legends of beings or creatures luring people to their deaths, and while most people dismissed them as just that, stories, I did not. Wilder believed in the magic of the prophecy, and now we know that magic is real. The stories of sirens luring sailors to their deaths had always intrigued me.

My family had lived along the coast in the Atlas Mountains. They had fled there as the water began to rise around the world. Before that, they lived in Marrakesh. My grandmother still had the old faded photos from the family albums. When I was little, she would show them to me, whispering words in the language of our people. We were isolated from the world, living a blessed life.

It made us unprepared for the attack.

They came for our figs and olives. They came for the oil we pressed. Our men had traded it once a year, traveling to the other side of the mountain to do it. I found out much later that they had been followed home. Our lives had been sold for another village's safety.

My life had been traded for another's.

I understand why—a parent is supposed to protect their child. I just wish... I don't bother finishing the thought, for it has never done me any good to wish or consider the what-ifs.

I was not on the King's ship first. Instead I was on another. Another that was lost at sea. I was the only one from that ship that survived. Unfortunately, the ship had been on course to rendezvous with the Black Death, so I was found by the King. He had questioned me about the night of the wreck. I told him about the singing, about the beautiful voice I had heard, and it had earned me a beating.

I had cried that first night, thinking there could be nothing worse than the beating.

I was wrong.

"This way, I think." Reyna's words slam the door on the dark memories threatening to swallow me whole. "Yes. Yes, this way."

She turns, her steps now taking us to the northeast, away from the path the stranger had given us.

"Are you sure?" I hate to question, but this new direction

has us moving away from Green Cove, away from my brothers.

"Yes. I know it sounds crazy, but we have to go this way. It's like the magic or power is moving. It's moving fast, racing in this direction." Her hand comes up pointing. "Do you trust me? Trust this magic you all have convinced me I have? The magic that is supposed to save us all?"

How do I argue with that? Haven't we been using the prophecy and who she might be to keep her with us? If we expect her to believe, then shouldn't I be willing to follow where that power is telling her to go?

"Yes. Lead the way." I reach out to take that hand and squeeze it and I'm gifted a smile that lights up her entire face.

She doesn't lose a second and starts jogging forward. I stay right at her side. We run for an hour at least, finally stopping when she is struggling for air.

"I think we are close, but it seems to have stopped." Reyna looks around once again, brow furrowed. She turns in half a circle then stops, facing north once again.

"Through the trees. I can hear the waves crashing. Whatever is calling is through there."

"I'll go first." I make sure my tone brooks no argument.

"Okay."

I'm half surprised she agreed so easily but I don't wait for her to change her mind. Starting forward, unlike Reyna, I move through the trees slowly, eyes roving over the area to watch for any sign of traps or ambush. I see nothing but I can't ignore the feeling of being watched.

"Are the wolves still with us?"

It is an innocent enough question she asks but it lets me know just how in tune to me she is. She is beginning to know our moods. I heard Fallon and Hagen whispering about Reyna, about how she is meant to complete each of us. Hell, I had the same thought as she welcomed me into her arms.

Knowing and understanding are two completely different things.

"I don't know. Maybe," I answer her question, hoping to reassure her, and a part of me is hoping she is.

'If you are still there, watch over her. Watch over us.' I send the thought out to whoever or whatever might be out there.

The light is beginning to filter through the trees, and I know we are almost free of the forest. We are almost to whatever is drawing us to the area.

Step by step, we walk into the unknown.

Abruptly sunlight blinds me. The sun has risen while we were ensconced within the branches of the forest. She stops at my side; we both blink rapidly as our eyes water from the brightness.

My vision is still blurry from the tears when I hear her cry out. "Cyder!" She jerks her hand from mine.

"Cyder?" I start running as I see the shock of red hair in the grass beyond Reyna's body. I run past her, flying to my brother's form. "Cyder!"

Tears race down my face as I slide to his side on my knees. He is still and pale, and I hold my breath, unwilling to face what might be true. I reach out slowly and before I can even touch his skin, I can feel the heat.

"Is he?" Reyna's voice cracks.

"He's alive but burning up." She falls to her knees across from me. I didn't even see her move.

"Oh my God, what happened to him?" Her fingers feather over the angry burn that is running down his body. "Would the King do this?"

"No. Not this. He would have kept him, tortured him. This... This is someone or something completely different." I lean down closer to my brother's face. "Cyder."

He doesn't respond, not that I actually thought he would, but I had that tiny glimmer of hope that his lids would raise and I would see the brilliance of his emerald eyes.

"He will die if we don't get him somewhere and get him help."

She's right, but how are we going to haul him to Green Cove? It's still two days walk, at least, and I'm afraid carrying him will do more harm than good.

I hear a rustling in the trees as she leans close to Cyder's face, whispering in his ear. Her words are so low that I can't hear them as I look around once again, searching for danger. The noise grows louder, and I know whatever it is out there is coming straight for us. Standing, I put myself between the two of them and the danger. My body tenses as I drop into a fighting position and slide the two blades that are stuck in my boots from their sheaths. I hold them loosely tucked back along my wrists and forearms. Waiting.

My breath escapes as Liam bursts through some undergrowth.

"Liam," Reyna cries, and I can hear the relief in her voice. "How did you find us?" She asks when he barrels into her, licking over her neck and face.

After a moment, he drops down to his belly and lets out a short howl. Something on her face makes the hair on my neck raise. She looks around, and I follow her searching eyes.

I wait, knowing she will speak eventually.

"He was drawn, just like I was. Something wanted us to find Cyder." There is so much conviction in her voice that I have no choice but to believe her words. "Quick, go look for some branches or fallen trees that we can use to build a carrier for him."

I start to question how we will join them but stop as she pulls the loose shirt over her head, leaving her in nothing but a tight undershirt that is molded to her breasts, like my hands were not too long ago. Lust threatens to take control, but I force it down and run for the trees, praying what we need is there. I can hear the fabric ripping but don't turn to look at her again.

I find one young sapling fallen and hack at another with my knife until I can push and break it the rest of the way through. It has long thin branches, and I think they are supple enough to be woven around the other trunk. Between the foliage and her fabric, we might just be able to do what we need to save Cyder.

Dragging the wood behind me, I enter the clearing to find Liam sniffing Cyder and then licking at his chest. He whines as he lifts his head and looks around. What is he searching for?

Reyna kneels at the poles I've dropped and then, like I had thought she would try, begins to wind the branches together until I notice a tightly woven pattern emerging.

I was not expecting her to begin to glow again as she was doing it, as she was so focused on saving him that she didn't even realize the green wood was bending to her will, growing and twisting itself to form something that resembles a hammock. I was not expecting the wind to pick up and lift long tendrils of her hair into the air. I was not expecting that faint glow I had witnessed this morning to brighten as flowers grew and bloomed all around us.

I did not expect magic.

She finishes and sits back, her eyes widening as she looks around us.

"What?"

She doesn't say more, doesn't need to.

"You." I can't keep the pride from deepening my voice.

"If I did that, then why can't I heal him?" She seems upset.

"Reyna, don't. You are saving him by getting us to help. And maybe someday you will be able to heal us, but for now, this is enough. Come on, beastie, let's get you hooked up." I wave Liam over, and he surprises me by moving right to the poles and backing up until he is between the front of them, just waiting to carry Cyder to help. "Why am I surprised?" I shake my head.

This time, I pull my shirt and take the remains of her fabric and tie pieces to the poles and the dog until I fashion a harness of sorts.

Reyna squats by Liam's head, her fingers scratching over his erect ears that are usually swiveling but have stopped to allow her access.

"I thought I had lost you." Tears moisten her cheeks. "I can't lose you. I can't lose him either. Are you ready to help me save him?" As if to answer, he licks away the tears and stands.

"Go slow, big guy," I warn as he begins to pull.

Cyder moans as the sled jerks when Liam pushes hard into the strap, forcing the wood to move.

"Easy." I lay my hand on Liam's back, and as the sled starts to glide over the ground, he begins a steady pace. "Good boy."

"Very good boy." Reyna beams from where she is walking beside Cyder, his hand in hers. "Do you think we will make it to help?"

Help. We will only save him if we make it to the rendezvous. I try to remember if there are any villages between us and Green Cove, but none come to mind. I'm still running over the coast between us when Liam shifts direction.

"No. We need to go this way." I try pulling him back on course, but he refuses. As a matter of fact, he doesn't even acknowledge that I had pulled at him. I feel the ripple of his muscles under my palm and once again realize just how massive the animal is. Looking over his back, I focus on Reyna. "Where did you say you got Liam?"

"I didn't really get him or find him. He found me. I was under a tree, reading and crying about some harsh words some kid said to me. He walked right up to me. Liam was big already but still had the gangly movements of a puppy. You know, where they sorta trip over their own feet? He just came up and laid at my side. He hasn't left me since." She rubs his shoulder, which is higher than her waist. "He is my very best friend."

"Do you think he was maybe sent to you?"

"I didn't before but now... Maybe. I've always known he was special. Different." She looks at his face, tongue hanging out even though I can tell he isn't working hard to pull my brother. "But now, I wonder if maybe..." She pauses a sweet smile curving her strawberry lips. "He's magical."

"I'm wondering the same thing. Animals have changed since the war. Adapted. But Liam is something altogether different. I thought at first maybe he was some sort of wolf or wolf-dog mix but now I just think he's more."

"Yeah, more. That's exactly it."

"Just like you," I say, and she glances at me, her cheeks pink.

Liam is leading us close to the coast and north, keeping us within sight of the water.

The sound of the waves settles some of the turmoil that has been churning within me. Until that is I see a sail in the distance. A sail that sends a tremor through my body.

"Down," I whisper at her, trying to catch hold of her arm to pull her to me. "Liam."

His ear swivels, but he keeps moving, shifting his trajectory slightly so that he is in the edge of the treeline. If anything, he picks up speed. Cyder cries out but falls silent after, sweat coating his skin. The fever is getting worse.

"Who is it?" Reyna's voice is filled with fear, and the sound of it is what stops Liam.

He looks back at his mistress.

"It is one of the King's ships but it is heading south, away from where my brothers should be." I shake my head.

They are in the canal, so they shouldn't be heading south. They should be chasing our ships. My heart starts pounding.

No.

No.

Reyna's head shaking is the only thing that alerts me to the fact that I had said the word out loud.

"They are safe. He didn't get them," she says, but I can tell she doesn't truly believe it.

Another ship, one that makes my skin crawl, comes into view. Two days have passed and I might have lost my family.

"Let's go," I say and cringe at how hard my voice sounds.

She stands and races toward Liam, and we all continue to run at the edge of the trees, no longer caring if we are seen. I keep my eyes on the water. We run for an hour before I stumble to a stop.

The channel has been closed. Who did it? The King or Hagen?

We race around the curve of the coast, following after the beast racing in front of us.

My heart stops.

CHAPTER SEVENTEEN
REYNA

*F*ive ships float in the water just off the coast, four circled around one, and my heart stutters then pounds with joy. They are safe.

Liam rushes ahead, turning toward a path that I didn't even see until he was on it, a tiny animal trail that runs precariously down the cliff face.

"Liam, slowly," I call, and he slows enough for me to catch up with them.

I shimmy by the makeshift carrier and move to his head, knowing Lash will stay at the rear to make sure the carrier and Cyder stay on the path. We begin to inch our way down, barely clearing an inch on both sides of us.

"Oh no," I cry out as I notice the sails are raised. "They are leaving."

"They won't hear us yelling," Lash growls, his eyes locked on the ships. "The wind is blowing, and Hagen's wolves are whining."

I can feel tears spring to my eyes and I scrub at them. I've always hated that I cry when my frustration gets the better of me. Liam bumps against me, and I look down, locking eyes with my friend.

His intelligence shines through as he studies me then turns his face toward the ships. A sound like nothing I've heard bellows out from his upturned muzzle. No, that's not true; it sounds like what woke me from my sleep. It sounds like the call that rang out through the forest, the sound that evoked both fear and calm within me. Staring at him, I feel the same again.

My special boy, where did you come from?

"They are turning." Lash's voice is quiet and filled with apprehension.

Glancing back at him before turning my eyes to the water once again, I see he is now looking at Liam with a look that makes me uneasy. Fear. I shift without realizing that I am putting myself between him and Liam.

"He wouldn't hurt you," I admonish. "He did it to help us. To help Cyder." My voice is hard.

The wind picks up more, blowing my hair around my head and face. My fingers catch hold of some that whips across my mouth as I focus on the ships bouncing on wild waves I hadn't noticed before. Liam whines.

Blinking, I look down and realize my fingers are spread wide. I close them making fists. I breathe deep. Once. Twice. And then a third time, calming the anger that had suddenly been raging within me. Anger like nothing I had ever felt. Liam whines again, and I move to his head, rubbing my fingers over his ears, letting the heat of him soak into my ice cold skin.

The wind dies down, and I look out to see Lash's ship moving closer to the shore.

"Come on, my friend, let's get Cyder to his people," I murmur, but my thoughts are wandering already.

I don't like how out of control I felt. I don't like how

different that rage made me feel. I keep those feelings to myself, no need to worry Lash or any of the others.

"Reyna?" Lash's hand touches my shoulder.

Looking up at him, I realize we are at the edge of the water. He had stopped me from walking right in. Liam stopped a few feet back.

"Let's get you unhooked." I step away from Lash's hand and his narrowed eyes.

He doesn't ask, but I feel his eyes on me as I kneel and start untying the fabric from around Liam's chest. I suddenly feel overwhelmed, like everything that has happened since I found Fallon on my shore has caught up to me. I remain focused on Liam until I hear the paddles of the skiff in the water. Only when the wood runs up on the rocks do I turn. Lash has his back to me and his muscles are tight.

I've hurt his feelings but I just can't talk about it. Not yet. I don't understand it. Not the feelings or the anger, but I do think the anger allowed some of the magic in me to flow out without my control. I didn't miss the change in the wind as soon as I calmed.

It terrifies me, this power that has been unlocked, and it feels like I am losing myself.

Liam nudges me, and I look up and see they have Cyder loaded into the small boat and the crewman at the bow is holding out his hand. Lash is seated beside his brother, and I hesitate. The boat is loaded down, the waves dangerously close to the washing over the edge.

"Take them out and then come back for me, if you don't mind." My tone and my face give them no chance to argue. I need a few minutes to gather my thoughts and get my emotions under control.

I give Lash a tiny smile, well, barely a smile, but he nods once at me then again at the men who have turned to look at him after my request. Liam sits down at my side, leaning into me, and as soon as the little boat is far enough away, I let the tears that have been barely held at bay flow.

Maybe it is being on land or alone for the first time in days, but my feelings are like a leaf blowing in a storm. I feel untethered to my own life.

Lost in a sea of death and destruction.

I am bringing more danger to these men. Cyder had almost been killed. Hagen was hurt. Who will be next?

Liam rests his head on top of mine, reminding me I'm not alone.

"I don't think I can do this," I whisper.

He stands and turns toward the cliff, ready to leave with me. Ready to keep me safe as he has always done.

"Thank you, my dear friend." I reach for him as I stand, facing away from the water. "The one called Nestor is wrong. I am not the one to save the world. I can't even save myself." I take a step toward the cliff and yelp when fingers close around my arm.

"Are you leaving me?" Hagen's deep voice is right behind my ear, his hot breath curls along my neck. "Leaving us?"

"I can't do this." I don't look back at him, but my body relaxes as he moves closer still and his other arm comes around my waist.

"What can't you do? Save the world or stay with me?" The last word is deeper, and he moves so that it vibrates the sensitive shell of my ear.

"Both. I put you all in danger." I try to stiffen, to strengthen the resolve that he is melting.

"We know nothing but danger. He has hunted us since he realized we didn't die in the water." Hagen tightens his hold. "I won't force you to stay. It is and always will be your choice." He closes his teeth over the tendon that runs along the side of my neck, and my head falls back of its own accord.

He is temptation personified. My dark captain. The one that calls to desires I didn't know I had.

"Not force. Right," I murmur when Hagen finally releases my neck.

"I didn't say I wouldn't fight, just that I wouldn't force. I will use every weapon in my arsenal." He pulls me around, making me face him.

Face my fear.

His finger moves under my chin, tipping my head back so that my eyes meet his. Then that same finger slides down my throat, stopping at the indentation at the base of my neck. I am fascinated both by the thought of his weapons and exactly how he would use them, but Hagen steps back, leaving me feeling unanchored once again. I realize he doesn't need to do anything. I will not leave. I can't leave them, for I have already fallen for them. My heart has split itself into five parts. I fear I will be lost without them.

"You chose us," he starts then pauses, and I hold my breath as he gathers his thoughts. "You chose us but you didn't get a chance to choose the magic. You had this whole 'save the world' thing shoved down your throat." I look to the side, and he lets me. "Know you will be my queen and I will follow you wherever you lead. We can forget the world and just sail. I will take you to see wonders like you can't imagine —the ice of the north and the jungles of the south."

He offers the world.

"You would leave them?" The words come out harsh as I look to the ships bobbing on the waves.

"No, they will follow you. If you don't want to fight. If we would have to run for the rest of our lives." He pushes my hair away from my face before cupping my cheek. "We have chosen you."

He leans close, giving me a chance to turn away, but I don't. Instead, I rise up, meeting his lips with my own. Unlike any of the others, he kisses me with no gentleness. I open for his onslaught, letting his fire burn and ignite my own. I feel my darkness reaching for his; I'm not scared. He devours me, drawing all of the rage and fear into him, taking it from me.

Giving me peace all while creating a storm within me.

We break apart gasping. My lips feel swollen and my heart is pounding. His eyes are half closed, but I see his hunger.

"What do you wish to do, dove?" His voice sounds like a storm.

"Dove?" Ducking my head, I hide the smile the pet name has conjured.

"A graceful but strong creature like you... Shall we run or fight?" Hagen asks my wishes once again, making it my choice.

"Take me to your ship. I know I was fooling myself thinking I could just run away from all of this. You were right—I chose you all and I chose to see where this journey takes us. I just..." I swallow away the emotion that threatens to choke my words. "I was afraid. I don't want to lose every-thing again."

"I won't promise you everything will be okay. I won't even tell you we will all survive, but we will all stay by your side until the moment we can't any longer. I will stand by you, so if your wings get broken, I will carry you until you can fly again."

Tears pool in my eyes, and I move into his arms, letting him hold me tight as I cling to him. He holds me until the tears slow then finally stop.

"How did you get chosen to come ashore?" I ask as I lean back and wipe my face.

"I was on my way before you even chose to stay on shore." He takes my hand and starts to lead me to the boat that is floating at the edge of the water. "Let's get you and your beast home."

"Home," I say on a sigh as I step forward.

Liam is in the boat before either of us. Hagen holds my hand as I step in and sit down on the seat. He then shoves us out a little before jumping in and taking up the oars. He rows smoothly and we glide over the water, which is now calm and glass-like. Eerily calm. I feel my nerves building once again and stick my hand down to touch the water, to feel the magic. At once, the nerves settle. Maybe the water and my captains' ships really are home.

Suddenly, Liam stands, ears perked and eyes on the cliff, or maybe the trees at the top. I scan but can't see anything.

"What is it, Liam?"

His only answer is a gravelly whine. He watches until we get to the ship. He watches as we are raised up on ropes. Leaping out, he runs along the deck eyes still on the trees.

"Hagen, something is watching us," I murmur, not wanting to alarm the crew.

"I know." He glances toward the shore. "But he doesn't seem to think it's a threat."

"Maybe it is the woman," I say, more to myself, but he hears and frowns.

"What woman?"

"Later. Right now, I want to check on Cyder." I start to the other side of the ship, hand reaching for the rope that will carry me to Cyder's side.

Hagen is right at my side as I reach it. "How bad is it?"

"Extremely." I grab the rope and take a few steps back then run forward, flinging myself across.

I reach the other side, and Fallon is there to catch me.

CHAPTER EIGHTEEN
CYDER

I'm drifting in a sea of pain.

Images dance through my mind, images of things I don't understand. Death and fire, screams and darkness. Fear crawls over my burnt skin. I see red eyes in the darkness and I feel the rub of hot fur over that same burnt skin.

Then suddenly, I feel something like a cold breeze skim over my body. I hear a whispered plea.

"Come back to me." Reyna's voice is strained but it beckons me.

I imagine I can feel her pulling me from the darkness, setting me free from the pain. Fallon calls out and I know I've been saved but I can't claw my way up to the light. I feel tethered somehow to the darkness. Tethered to death.

I wonder if it's because of who tried to kill me, or who I think tried to save me. It could be that I was actually dead and I'm now linked to the realm of the dead. I would have never considered anything of the sort before but now after seeing so many unusual things, I wouldn't be surprised.

That coolness washes over me again and the tether pulls

tight. It stretches but doesn't snap. I fear that even if I find my way back to my brothers and Reyna, I will never break free from this place.

I thought I could feel no worse pain than I have but suddenly, I know I'm wrong. A scream is torn from my throat and the light comes rushing. I'm blinded by the brightness of the sun and I can't stop the screaming that is coming from me.

"Cyder." Just my name said gently in my ear.

I force the scream to stop, locking my jaw shut and roll my eyes to Reyna's face. Her blue eyes are filled with concern and a hint of relief.

"My queen." My voice has been shredded by my screams and doesn't sound like my own.

"My captain." She kisses my cheek. "I was afraid." She doesn't finish, her eyes filling with tears.

"I wouldn't let some fucking bitch goddess kill me," I growl but it doesn't sound at all as tough as I wanted it.

"Goddess?" Fallon leans his face into view.

"Later, Fallon." She sounds like the queen we have crowned. "We need to get under way. We need to get him a doctor."

"Reyna, it's okay. We have doctors," Wilder says from somewhere to my left. I don't bother looking. "They are all coming."

"Kellihan has sent you food. I wouldn't tell Cyder's cook, though; he might be offended that the old coot doesn't think his food is good enough for you," Fallon jokes, but I see the fear on his face.

"Yes, Reyna. You should eat. We ran for miles, and you haven't eaten in a couple days." Lash is at my feet.

"How did I get here?" I moan as pain rips through me again.

"Reyna and Lash found you," Fallon responds.

"Reyna found you," Lash corrects him, and my eyes stay on her face.

"I did nothing but follow..." she pauses, her brows drawing down, "the call or beacon. I don't know how to describe it."

"Magic." I try to smile but I'm afraid I fail as my ship's doctor touches the blistered flesh on my chest.

"A goddess burned you?" Fallon asks, his eyes on the doctor's fingers, which have been joined by another's.

I squeeze my eyes closed and fight to drag a breath in, but the pain... "Fuck, Douglas, you are killing me," I grunt.

"There is nothing we can do for the burn—it is deep and will leave a horrible scar, Captain—but we can get the infection and fever under control. I am concerned about the damage under the burn." He glances at the other doctors. "Can you tell us how exactly you were hurt?"

Coughing, I try to laugh but again I don't quite manage it. "A goddess stole me from the King and when she got to know me, she cut me right up the middle."

A gasp draws my eyes back to Reyna. "Then she burned you?" Her voice makes me want to hold her, but instead, I just squeeze her hand.

'No. That was from a beast that makes Liam look like a pup. She was frightened of it. I couldn't fight it off, although I realized quickly enough that I think it was trying help. It sniffed me and then licked over the wound and, boom, charred meat." I don't mention the holding in my guts part.

"We will need to keep a very close eye on you. You could be bleeding inside. We may need to open you up," Fallon's doctor informs me and those standing at my side.

I can only nod and pray that it doesn't come to that. "We need to get these ships moving." I look at Hagen, who jerks his head then whistles.

A flurry of movement takes place around me, and I

realize I am lying on my own deck. Travis steps into view, his eyes downcast.

"I'm sorry, Captain, we... I failed you."

"No, Travis, you always serve me well." I shake my head and grimace at the slight movement pulling at my flesh.

"We had traitors, spies, on our ships, brother." Fallon sits at my side while our other brothers move away to their own ships. "They have been dealt with, but we are still trying to figure out how they are communicating."

"Can we discuss this later? He needs to rest." Reyna once again doesn't leave any room for argument.

"I will return to the Rose. Be well, Cyder." He rises and nods at Reyna before doing just as he said.

We are alone and I feel exhaustion trying to pull me away from her. "Sleep, my Captain, I will be here when you wake," she promises.

"I feel as if I have been asleep for entirely too long. I dreamt of death and darkness and I'm not yet ready to return. Tell me a story, my queen."

"I could read to you from one of your books," she offers and I nod.

I watch as she rises and then makes her way to my cabin. She returns in moments with the book of Celtic myths in her hands, and I actually manage to smile this time. I let my eyes close as she begins to speak, reading tales of the old gods, the gods that are at this very moment meddling in our lives.

The ship begins to move, and I can hear the sails as they catch the wind and snap tight to propel us away from the coast. Reyna's voice dies away, and I hear the sound of the book closing.

"You scared me." Her voice is tight when she finally speaks after a long silence.

"I was afraid they were hunting you and Lash on shore." I

hold out my hand, and a moment later, her fingers slide against my palm then thread with mine.

"Liam hunted you and we had a few guards the first night."

I hear wonder in her voice and open my eyes to study her face. "Guards?"

"A pack of wolves." She grins at whatever she sees on my face. "Lash is certain I called them to us somehow, although I have no idea how. That's the problem, though. If I have some power, I have no idea how to make it an asset to us in this fight."

"Miss?" Reyna glances away from me. "I've brought you some food and some broth for the Captain."

"Thank you." She smiles and I see how tired she looks before she turns back to me. "Here, let me get a pillow for under your head." She starts to stand, but I squeeze her hand.

"I want to move into my quarters but I'm afraid I can't stand."

"You better not even try." She scowls then looks around. "Excuse me. Your captain needs to be moved into his own bed."

I hear the pounding of feet before she even finishes asking. Travis's face comes into my view, and as he watches my face, the crew lifts me slowly and much more gently than their menacing expressions demand.

"Careful," Reyna murmurs as I grimace from the slight jostling.

"I'm fine," I assure her, even as I feel sweat bead on my face and shivers begin to rack my body.

She notices, as does Travis.

"Doc!" He yells and more feet pound across the deck as they shift me to my own bed, the beautiful picture hanging across from me.

"Cover his lower body and bring blankets to tuck around him," Doc tells the young crewman helping him.

I'm fighting to not cry out at the pain coursing through me. The doctor feathers his fingers over the wound, and I grip the sheets in my fist.

"I am going to put some ointment on this burn, and it will hurt." He grimaces as I nod.

Reyna squeezes my hand as the other crewmen leave the room, leaving just her and the doctor. Travis is last out and he closes the door, leaving me to a new torture. I squeeze my eyes shut as the ointment is spread down my midline. My muscles are shaking uncontrollably, and my body is soaked.

"I'm glad you are sweating," Doc mumbles as he wipes his hand on an apron hanging around his neck. "If you stop, you are in trouble." He looks at Reyna. "You must make sure he drinks and gets as much broth down his throat as you can, my queen." He nods then stands. "I will leave this here, and you can apply some in a few hours."

He leaves us and I groan, finally able to release the breath I had been choking on. I have no shame that tears have leaked from my eyes. I wish I had passed the fuck out, for the medicine might be worse than the actual torture.

"I'm so sorry." Reyna's tears are evident in her voice, and I open my eyes, locking them on her face.

"This isn't your fault in any way. It is his fault. He has always been insane and he is becoming more so as the thing that we are all searching for calls to him, corrupting his already evil soul more." I lift my hand and wipe the tears from her left cheek. "Do you hear it calling to you? I have heard rumors of so many being drawn to the north."

"I hear nothing, but maybe if I knew how to unlock the magic everyone is sure I have, I could find it." She chews at her lower lip and shakes her head.

I don't think she realizes she is doing either.

"It's new and unknown. Just like anything else, it will take time. You can't rush it. As a matter of fact, I think this magic and the gods will only show us what they want, when they want. Maybe they are letting you get used to the idea of having a power before letting you have full access to the power. If it is supposed to be something that can save the world, I would think it's going to be something to behold." Talking to her has calmed her and also taken my mind off the pain for a few minutes.

"I guess you could be right. I just wish I knew what to even look for."

She shoves her hair back, revealing her neck, and I see a slight smudge of dark flesh. I can't stop my eyebrow from raising as I wonder what might have happened as she and Lash slept in the forest. A surge of jealousy courses through my belly, but I push it away. I am happy for my brother, and if any of us deserve to be held in her arms, it is Lash.

We might joke with him, but I know how much damage he suffered at the King's hands. Hagen and I suffered the King's need to inflict pain. Fallon and Wilder were tormented mentally with our pain, along with their own pain. Lash endured much worse things, things he will not speak of. I hope he finds some peace with Reyna.

I'm not completely unselfish though, because I wish the same for myself. I will have new nightmares to haunt my nights now. Nightmares of a bitch goddess and her shining blade. Hell, even the hound will haunt me. I'm still not sure it was helping me or claiming me for a meal. Testing my blood.

Reyna shifts, and I realize she has grown quiet while I was lost in the past. Now she's holding the bowl in one hand and the spoon in her other.

"Let's get some broth in you before it grows colder than it already is." She spoons some of the almost clear liquid and holds it to my lips.

We repeat the process until I grow tired. Holding up my hand, I stop her from scooping another spoonful and let my head relax back, letting my eyes close again.

"You should eat, yourself," I murmur as I feel sleep trying to pull me away from her.

Just as I begin to fall, images flash and my body jerks. Forcing my eyes open, I beat the images back, along with the tension that has tightened all my muscles. My body shakes with fear. I taste it on my tongue and I hate it. I haven't tasted it in a very long time. I know I will have the flavor of it in my mouth for a very long time to come. These creatures that are directing our destinies are unknown, powerful, and as far as I can tell, vicious, without a thought for how their actions affect us. Not just those of us on these ships, but humans in general.

The fear disappears instantly when she shifts slowly onto the bed, careful not to jostle me or touch my damaged skin. Her hand is cool as she lays it against the side of my neck, her thumb stroking over my collarbone.

"Are you warm enough?" She whispers, her forehead against my upper arm.

"I'm burning." I don't tell her it's like Hades himself has hold of my guts.

I had always liked the stories of the old gods, both the Greek and Celtic, but now they seem too real. I remember how vicious and punishing they were said to be, and my run-in with Nemesis proved that to be true.

But she is straightforward in her hatred; it is the other one that I truly fear. I can get no sense of his intentions. True, he has guided and still is, but has he helped? I fear we are nothing more than chess pieces to him. He moves us to win a game that we know nothing about.

A breeze blows over my burning flesh, ruffling my hair, and I look at Reyna. Her eyes are closed, brows pulled down low, and a slight glow is coming from her luminescent skin. I hold my breath, afraid to disturb her.

The light pulses and the breeze grows cooler, and I can feel a dampness on my skin. It's like a thick fog without the cloudiness. My ship begins to roll, and I know a storm is brewing outside.

Reyna begins to talk. Her words are so low I can't make them out, but they have a cadence to them. The door opens and I hold up my hand to stop Travis from speaking. His eyes glide over Reyna, seeing her for the goddess she is.

The thought stops me, making me widen my eyes.

I whistle low, just a hint of sound to let Travis know I need my brothers. He jerks his head and backs out, shutting the door without making a sound.

We were fine with a queen but a goddess with massive or even possibly unlimited power? That, I'm not sure about. Reyna, I could love, but if she changes into something different, something cold, would she love us? Would she care about any human?

I hear the call go out and the response. The storm that is blowing outside is one I think Reyna is creating with her power. Turning my head, I glance out the window above us.

"Sweetheart." I turn my face and graze the top of her head with my lips.

It does what I wish, breaking her concentration as she turns her face up to mine. She takes my lips in a hungry kiss, her hand sliding up to cup my jaw. Fingers add pressure, demanding I open for her, and I comply willingly. We kiss like only people who have almost lost each other can.

I'm so lost in the heat of her mouth that I don't feel the waves calm or the ship grow still. A knock at my door forces us apart, and I can't help but move in for one more kiss then I pull back, shocked. Not at the kiss but at the lack of pain from the movement.

"Oh my God." Her eyes are filled with curiosity and a hint of fear.

I follow her eyes and feel my own sense of fear, but mine is mixed with wonder. The coolness and moisture was healing me, had healed me, and I hadn't even known it. My finger traces over the horrendous raised and red scar that runs the length of my torso, but there is no pain.

"I just..." she stammers as she too reaches to touch my skin. "I was praying your fever would break. I didn't..." She stops and looks up, locking eyes with me again.

"Well, you certainly did that. Your body was, for lack of a better word, glowing, like a pearl in moonlight." I run my thumb over her reddened lips, trying to wipe away the fear still lurking in her eyes and replace it with the hunger that was burning so brightly in them only moments ago.

A harsher knock interrupts again, and without ever taking my eyes from hers, I call out, "Enter."

"Damn it, Cyder, it's pouring out here and you called us."

Hagen stomps in and Reyna pushes up but slides her hand down to mine. I can feel her body shaking.

"A little rain has never hurt you, Hagen." I smirk as I turn my face toward him and push up. My skin is tight but there is minimal pain.

"Holy shit." Fallon stops in his tracks. "What..." He stops and his eyes move to Reyna at my side.

Lash enters next. "Why didn't you..." He doesn't finish as Reyna jumps to her feet and races out of my room, shoving by all of them.

Wilder enters moments later as I pull on a clean shirt. "She went to Fallon's ship. Liam followed. It is unnerving how far that dog can jump at times." He shakes his head and closes the door behind him.

"She healed you?" Fallon asks, even though I can tell from his face he already knows the answer.

"She did but she has no idea how. In all honesty, I don't either, other than the glistening glow of her skin. She called the storm also." I glance out and see the clouds are dissipating.

The sun is bright and high in the sky. It is amazing but terrifying because it hints at what she might be capable of.

"She glowed when I woke this morning to her standing in the clearing, hands held out at her sides. It was after that she said something was calling her, and we walked straight to you." Lash tells us all. "I was going to tell you all when Cyder was well."

"Anything else you were waiting to tell us?" Hagen scowls at Lash, who suddenly looks uncomfortable.

"Lash." Fallon urges him to tell us whatever else he has been holding back.

"A woman. She found us in the forest and pointed us in this direction. Pointed us in the direction of Liam. I felt she truly wanted to help us. The way she told us was like someone just suggesting a direction because they knew the way ships traveled but it felt off to me." He shrugs. "I can't explain it any better."

"One of the old ones trying to guide us?" I say pacing away.

"Maybe." He nods.

"That's why I called you all here." I start but pause, unsure of exactly how to continue. I swallow as Nemesis's face flashes in my mind. "After meeting a goddess and now feeling a hint of the power growing in Reyna, I wonder if maybe we have to worry about her."

"Worry, how?" Wilder draws near me, watching me closely.

"I worry that the power might change her. We don't know what they are driving us to. The prophecy says she will save the world, but we don't know who she will save it for. The goddess Nemesis thought we were nothing, so much lesser that we don't deserve a second thought. I'm afraid we will lose our queen."

Hagen stiffens, as does Fallon. Wilder's head shakes, and Lash cries out.

"No."

"I'm not saying I'm sure of it. I'm saying we do not know what can or will happen. We have been set on this path and yet, we know nothing of the true nature of it. She is important to all of us. Becoming more so everyday." I lock eyes with Fallon and then Wilder.

Wilder is the keeper of the tales, the reader, the scholar. I hope he might have some ideas or remember a story. But he is silent.

"We cannot stop it." Hagen is the first to speak. "You said it yourself—she doesn't know how or even when she is using this power. It's growing, whether or not we want it to. Whether or not she wants it to. We are on this path. I don't think we can get off of it if we wanted to."

Fallon stays quiet, his fingers rubbing over his jaw. It is his tell, giving away his turbulent thoughts, because we all know the scar that hides beneath the short beard that covers it. It was a present from the King, made with a blade carved from bone. The infection had almost killed Fallon, and for the longest time, the scar had been raised and puckered. It's a constant reminder of his punishment, not only to him but to everyone that looked at him.

"It scares her as much or more than it does us. Prophecy or no, we have sworn to protect her, to stand with her. Power or no, she is our queen. Destiny or no, she is mine." Fallon looks around the room pausing on each of us.

"And mine." Lash's voice is filled with possessiveness.

"And mine." Wilder sounds as he always does, so sure of our future and our part in hers.

"Mine." Hagen sounds like the predator.

"Mine, also." I smile as I tilt my head slightly to the side.

"Then there is no reason to worry." Fallon turns and strides out, and I raise my brows.

We all stand silent for a moment.

"So... Was it all I think it will be?" I break the tense silence, looking at Lash.

"What?" Hagen glances between us.

"More." Lash grins as he spins away and leaves us both staring after him.

Laughter bubbles up from deep within me, and I can't stop it as Hagen stands confused and staring at me. The laughter is uncontrollable, a release of at least some of the tension that has been coiled in me since I was taken. I stop and swallow, looking at Hagen, and I notice he is watching me with concern.

I choose not to elaborate on my outburst and instead focus on our many problems.

"How did they find us?" Waving my hand, I ask him to join me in sitting.

"The spies." He frowns like it was a stupid question.

"Yes, I know that, but how?"

"We don't know exactly. We were about to question Jamie when we heard Liam's call." Hagen glances out the window. "I wonder if maybe one of our concerns shouldn't be exactly what Liam is, because I have a hard time believing he is of this world."

"I have wondered that myself since the day they joined us. Not the 'of this world' part, but the 'what is he' part... If I'm not mistaken, he is growing."

He nods. "Has Reyna noticed?"

"I can't be sure but I think she has been too distracted with everything else."

"Shall we go speak to Jamie?" He pushes up, finished with

our conversation. Hagen has always been one of few words, which is why we get along so well. "What was more?"

I grin. "What do you think?"

"Really?" His eyes widen and a small smile curves his lips. No jealousy like I had, just acceptance. "Good for him; he deserves it."

That is it, nothing more. Hagen thinks of himself as the worst of us all but in many ways, he is the best. He does not judge. He does not covet and never has. He began protecting us the moment he stepped on the ship. Hagen knows the worst of us and still only wants the best for us and will sacrifice anything to make sure we get it, even himself.

"I don't know Jamie well, but it doesn't seem like something he would do," I argue as I stand and follow him from my quarters. "Why would he do this?"

"The King has his sister. He is holding her on his ship."

I couldn't be more shocked and horrified at his revelation. "On his ship?"

Memories assail me. I see us broken, I hear our screams, and I taste our blood.

I would not wish it on my worst enemy.

"She is still a child. We don't have much time to save her and we have no idea how to do it." Hagen shakes his head, and for a moment, I see how tired he is.

"Then let's get to it." Reyna's voice startles me, and I spin to see her standing on my deck.

She has changed and looks less afraid. Hagen moves past me and nods at her then leads the way. She follows right behind him, and I come last. Jamie has been brought from Fallon's ship and looks utterly defeated when we reach him below deck. He is in a darkened room with nothing but a chair, which he is tied to.

"Release him," I tell Travis, who is at my back.

My first mate complies immediately. Jamie doesn't try to leave the chair; he has accepted his fate.

"Tell me how you let them know where we are," Hagen asks, and I'm surprised at his gentleness.

"Birds. There are birds on every ship. And we pick new ones up in ports when we have sent the ones we have," Jaime answers quickly.

I'm still pondering his answer when I realize Reyna is gone.

CHAPTER NINETEEN
REYNA

*J*realized something while I was sitting in Kellihan's kitchen. I can't be frightened of everything all the time.

I can't let fear control my destiny.

Running my fingers over the folded letter in my pocket, I remember its words. I remember the emotion behind them. Remy believed I could do this. Nestor believes I can do this.

Evil grows where there is no good.

I must be the good that stops it.

Where would they keep birds hidden on a ship full of crewmen? I walk and do the only thing I can think of. Drawing a deep breath, I look inside and try to release the magic within me.

For the first time, I am not scared of it. I feel embraced by it, and it is wondrous.

'Help me. If you want me to do this, you have to help me.'

It's a prayer to those that have sent me down this path. I feel, rather than see, the tendrils flowing from my body, feel them pulling me through the ship. The bird is in a small cage, a strap around its leg. Pen and page sit to the side, just waiting to carry a message to the one hunting me.

I don't know when but at some point, I've made a decision. It is one they will not like. One those who chose me for this mission will not like. But it is the only way forward I can think of right now. I don't know how to control this magic and I'm afraid it is controlling me.

If it can't save them, I can.

I pick up the pencil and write a short note then attach it to the bird.

"Fly well," I whisper as I throw it up into the air.

I watch out the opened port until it disappears. Now I just have to wait until nightfall.

I hear steps and turn, schooling my face. The boy named Jamie comes into view with Hagen and Cyder right behind him. They pause when they see me.

"It was empty when I found it. Could one of the others have released the birds?" I ask and pray that I sound believable.

Hagen narrows his eyes but says nothing. Cyder starts forward again, stopping at my side to look in the small cage.

"How could this have been missed by everyone on this ship?" His voice is hard. His emerald eyes gleam with anger and they land on the boy.

Jamie's voice is shaky when he answers. "The other spy was in charge of this area and he would move it if anyone else was going to be around here."

"It matters little now," Hagen quips. "They are all gone. The traitors and the birds, it would seem.

"I did want to see it though," Cyder grumbles before turning his hand and grabbing young Jamie's arm as he passes him.

I stand planted where I am watching him go, walking so soon after being close to death. It is a miracle, one I performed, and yet could I do it again if needed? I didn't do it for Hagen when his leg was cut open and the blood flowed from him. I glance at the very man still standing in the shadowed room with me. He has yet to speak, but even knowing him as little as I do, I know he has something on his mind. I didn't like how he looked at me as I lied. Turning, he starts to leave me, the limp from his wound still noticeable.

Two of my captains were hurt because of me. Because of what I represent to anyone looking for whatever is hidden.

"Reyna?"

I focus and see him watching me once again and I force a smile to my face.

"Coming." He waits as I walk forward to his side. "Is your leg getting better?"

"Much." His voice is strong, solid, and deep, reminding me of the dark of night. He doesn't seem to notice that his hand is rubbing gently over the wound. "Would you come to the Wolf?"

I shouldn't but then again, which ship should I go to? None are any better than the others for my plans. He just waits until finally I give in and nod. Hagen's rough hand takes my own, and we make our way through the belly of Cyder's ship.

Once on deck, I see the others have moved away, but the wolf is still sailing right alongside, the wind still howling through Hagen's wolves flying on his masts. They make an eerie sound but somehow they are soothing, maybe because of the guardians in the forest or maybe because of Liam. This ship might be exactly where I need to be today.

"I thought you might like to rest," he says by my shoulder as his crewman swings the rope over to us.

"I would like to lie down," I admit but I don't think sleep will come.

Nodding, he hands me the rope, letting me go first. I turn

S LAWRENCE

and look at Cyder, who is leaning against his door, his hand is pressed against his sternum. I see a flash of him doing the same, but this time, blood is gushing and his flesh is hanging open. I gasp and lose my balance. Hagen catches hold of me as I try to catch my breath. Cyder straightens and takes a step toward us, but I wave my hand and he stops.

"Sorry, I think I'm just more tired than I thought."

"Understandable. Get her to bed, Hagen," Cyder calls but he watches me closely.

They all do. They always are. It will make my plan even harder than it already is.

Hagen jumps up beside me and wraps his arm around my waist, holding me tight as he swings us both across. The feeling of him wrapped around me as we glide through the air is indescribable. He makes me feel safe. I blink away tears as our feet hit the deck.

"Come." His hand slides to my hip and he keeps me tucked against his side as he guides me to his quarters.

He opens the door for me then turns back to his first mate. I don't wait to hear the conversation because it matters little to me what plans they make. I hear Liam bark and I smile; I'm glad my friend has followed me. I wait just inside until he rubs against me and I don't fail to notice that he is changing too.

What is fate doing to us?

"Come, my friend, let's lie together for a while." I try not to let my emotions overwhelm me, but Liam knows me too well.

He pushes and whines, forcing me forward. I go willingly. I had thought I couldn't sleep but I feel it pulling at me. We will both need our rest.

"I'm going to need you tonight," I murmur as I lay down and smile as he curls beside me, his massive head laying over my hip as he watches the door. "He will watch us and keep us

180

safe. Rest, my friend." A grumbling growl is his only response, but just as I feel myself falling, his body relaxes.

The sun is getting low when I wake. Liam is gone and in his place is Hagen. He has covered me with a dark cover and is sleeping at my back, protecting me like I knew he would. My throat clogs with my emotions, and I swallow hard.

"Ready for some food?"

I close my eyes as desire floods my system at the sound of his deep voice, thick with sleep. His hand tightens on my hip where it is laying. I roll, enjoying the feel of his hand sliding over my body. His eyes are half closed, but I can see the golden flecks in the mahogany darkness. The golden matches the highlights in his blonde hair. The sun shining on it right now turns it into spun gold.

The paleness of his appearance is so at odds with the darkness of the surroundings and his personality. He looks like what I imagined of a vampire in an old book I had once found and read. The vampire had been called Lestat and much like Hagen, he ruled those around him while looking like a beautiful statue. He had also had golden blonde hair. That is where the resemblance ends though. If I am truthful, I fell half in love with that vampire and I'm falling for this one also.The thought makes me smile, and I watch as his brows draw together in question. My hand floats up and I cup his smooth cheek as I shake my head once before tilting my head back, beckoning him.

His eyes flare bright as he crashes into me. That is Hagen, my fiery captain. He is like the storms that rock the ships, the lightning that lights the sky. He is a force that you can't contain, so you just hold on.

I hold tight.

He kisses me like a tsunami, and the force of his desire reshapes me in my soul. I realize that before he had just been playing, but now he was serious in his need of me. I open to his onslaught, letting him wash away my fear of what I must do. He kisses me until I am breathless and my body is on fire. His flames are burning me, branding me.

Finally, he pulls back, biting my lower lip and pulling it with him. I go liquid with need. Releasing it, he rubs over that lip with his thumb. My eyes flutter open and I see a promise etched in his face.

"How about a bath first?"

His question throws me. My lust-addled brain can't even process it for a moment, and I stare at him dumbfounded as he smirks. It's a smirk of a man who knows exactly what he's done.

"A bath?" He nods as he pushes up, his fingers sliding over my neck and pausing at the pulse pounding there.

"Yes." He looks behind me, so I turn my head. There in the dark corner sits a round wooden tub.

A sigh escapes my lips when I think about a bath. It feels like it has been years since I've had one. I nod as I turn back to him. He has stood and now he crosses to the door. Opening it, he calls out to someone called River. Just two words.

"Now, River."

He had planned it while I slept. My heart softens.

"Where is Liam?" I notice he isn't in the room.

"I lured him away with food and I'm sure Cook is still feeding the beast." His golden hair gleams as he shakes his head.

Moments later, the door is pushed wide as a string of men carry in buckets of steaming water.

"How?" At home, we have to heat it all over a fire.

"Solar heater. We found the instructions in one of the books from the city. It took me longer to find some solar panels that hadn't been destroyed by the war or time."

The sound of the water pouring forced my body into

motion. It took the men no time to empty their buckets and leave.

"Do all the ships have one?" I ask as I move to the tub.

"No. They all have showers based on the same principle, but only I have the tub."

I can picture him in it, the steam curling the hair around his temple.

"It gets cold quickly so..." he trails off, and it's my turn to smile slyly.

I unbutton my shirt, pushing it off my shoulders and letting it fall. Next comes my pants, which I untie and push down over my hips. I straighten and look right at my captain. I like the lust I see on his face and I love the way his fists are clenching and unclenching.

I feel bold.

I don't let myself think twice. Instead, I slide the bra and panties that had come from Lash off and let them drop beside the other things. I stand for a moment, letting his eyes devour me. Then I turn and step into the hot water, sinking slowly until I'm covered. At some point, my eyes have closed, and when I open them, he is beside me.

My heart stutters when he kneels. I watch as he picks up a pitcher and dips it in the water, then I close my eyes as he tips my head back and pours it over my hair. He repeats the process until all of my hair is wet. A sigh escapes when he begins to lather the wet strands. The room is filled with his scent and steam. He is washing me with his soap. Again a brand, a claim, and I relish it.

After rinsing it, he drapes my hair over the edge. My eyes are still closed when his hand begins to glide over my arm, moving up to my shoulder then across my collarbone. He is behind me, and I can feel his stomach against my head as he reaches both hands down. Rough skin moves over my smoothness as he cups my breasts, the soap making them slick. I arch my back, pressing into his palms. He squeezes tighter, kneading as my heart beats faster. Then they are gone and moving down under the water across my stomach, as the muscles there flutter in anticipation.

"I have dreamt of this since before we found you." His breath is warm at my ear, and I shiver at the darkness I hear in it. "Dreamt of ruling someone here in my room. Would you let me rule you, my queen?"

I swallow as his teeth close on the tendon in my neck, causing me to shiver again.

"Yes."

One hand glides back up my body and closes around my neck, tightening slightly, just a hint of pressure, but it causes moisture to flood my core as he forces my face to his.

"Open your eyes, my queen. I want to see your eyes. I want you to see me." I do as he demands, locking my green gaze with his golden one.

His other hand plunges down, spreading my lips to gain entrance to my core, and I gasp as he thrusts in. Just a single finger, but that is all it takes. Crashing in for another kiss, he swallows my gasp. His tongue thrusts into my mouth just like his finger is thrusting into me, and my fingers curl over the edge of the tub, trying to hold on. Once, twice, three times his finger moves in and out of me. Then it is gone. He moves higher, rubbing gently over the nub that is throbbing with need.

Still he kisses me, eating all of my moans until he breaks away. His hand leaves me and I open my eyes, focusing on him once again.

"Stand."

It is an order, and he watches me closely. This is it, no going back, but the darkness beckons. I am supposed to be something for each of them but I know they are each something different for me. Hagen is a place to free the darkest of my desires, desires I didn't know I had until I was in his arms. No, that's not true. He has called to me from the moment I saw him on Cyder's ship.

"I said stand, my queen." Fingers lace through my hair and he pulls.

Not hurting but skating that line, and any fear I had hiding within me evaporates. He senses it. A smile curves his lips as I stand, and he pulls my head back to kiss me hard.

Hagen lifts me from the water then turns, walks the few steps to his bed, and tosses me on it.

I am on display for him and I start to close my legs, but a growl from him stops me.

"You do what I say in here. I am your king." The words and the tone heat my blood even more. "In here, I am your everything."

He stares at me from the foot of the bed, waiting.

"Yes," I whisper.

He grabs my ankle, pulling me closer to the edge, then runs his fingers up my leg, his short nails scratching, raising goose bumps all over my body. My skin is cool with the dampness of the water, and his hands feel like brands. I don't know when he started touching my other leg, but now he grips my knees, spreading me, devouring me with his eyes.

"Do not move." An order.

I watch as he kneels, his shoulders between my knees, bracing them apart. His fingers curve on my thighs, moving up until he reaches the apex. Then he leans forward, his eyes on mine as his breath blows over my core.

I shiver and bite my lip.

"I'm going to show you who you really are," he growls, and for the second time, I am shaken.

CHAPTER TWENTY

HAGEN

*S*he truly is a queen.

A queen that I will rule.

I have dark desires, and her willingness to indulge them soothes something in me. I will rule her in here, in this place, but in every other sense, she will rule me. I give myself to her willingly, just as she is giving herself to me now.

My shoulders keep her legs spread, keep her open to me, as I lean forward. I watch her face as I speak, watching her pupils dilate.

"I'm going to show you who you really are."

She bites her lip as I move the last inch, letting my lips touch the moisture coating her, a mixture of water and her own juices. Moving back slightly, I let her watch as I lick over my lower lip. She tastes like honeyed wine, a heady mixture that goes straight to my head.

I'm going to get drunk on her. She will become my addiction.

Her hips shift slightly in an unspoken plea. Instead of giving her what she wants, I shift over her, dragging my tongue up her stomach to the underside of her breast. One hand comes up and I run it over her left breast, the full mound of it filling my hand as I knead it. Still I watch her face.

How far can I push her?

I test her desires, test her limits.

Squeezing her breast harder, I then roll the taut nipple between my thumb and forefinger. Her eyes widen slightly then the lids fall to half mast. I squeeze it harder as I lick over the right nipple then draw it into my mouth. She arches into both, her breath catching. I suck on the flesh hard and pinch the other harder and she moans.

She is beautiful in her need.

I let her nipple slide from my lips. "I want to do bad things to you."

"Yes," she answers, feeding my need.

I move back down her body slowly until I'm kneeling once again. She frowns but I don't give her what she wants. Not yet. Instead, I grab her and flip her over, smiling at her gasp. Her gorgeous ass is right in front of me, and I run my hands over it, feeling the smoothness.

Her body starts to relax, and before she can recognize what is happening, I raise my hand and bring it down hard. The sound of my palm hitting her flesh makes my cock harder than it already was. The pale creaminess turns pale pink.

I lean down and run my tongue through the fresh wetness that is coating her pussy. She pushes back against my mouth, and I use my other hand to slap her other cheek. Then I begin to devour her, thrusting my tongue in and out, biting with my teeth, pushing her pain and pleasure. Sliding my hand, I move my mouth slightly, just enough to hook my thumb inside her then start to lick over her again. Flicking the hard numb, I push her as I feel her begin to quiver.

I slide my other hand up along her spine and grab the

dark hair there, pulling her head back and forcing her back to arch. It raises her ass, giving me better access. I take full advantage, shifting so I can replace my thumb with two fingers. I pump them in and out while sucking on her clit. She is panting. Shaking.

"Hagen," she cries, begging. "Please."

"Not yet." I pull her hair harder but pull my mouth away, letting her come down.

She whimpers, pushing back with her hips. My fingers are still buried deep within her, and I feel her muscles clenching around them.

"Please."

I relish the tone, the submission.

"On your knees."

She moans as she complies, and I remove my hands just long enough to undo my pants and shove them down. I want her too much to take my time. I push her forward on the bed as I rise up. She stays on her knees as I move behind her.

Curving over her, I whisper in her ear, "I can't be slow so instead, I'm going to be hard and fast."

"Yes."

"Good." I kiss her between her shoulder blades then line my cock up with her entrance.

Rising up, I look as I run my dick over her, wetting it. She pushes back, but I place my hand in between her shoulders and push her upper body down, raising her ass even more. Then I thrust in hard, burying myself in one move. She cries out, the pleasure too intense.

I pull out and thrust forward again. My hands grip her hips, holding her in place. I pound into her over and over until she is chanting my name and pushing back into me, making every thrust harder.

Taking one hand, I reach around and pinch that erect nub. She screams as the orgasm rushes through her, surprising her, and her muscles clamp down on me like a vice. I pound harder until I feel fire burning up my legs. I come in her, my cock flexing as her muscles milk me. I collapse, pulling her down with me, and we lay like that—me locked within her, our breathing ragged.

The sun is setting as I reach around and roll her nipple in between my fingers once again and growl as her muscles clench on me.

"Hagen." She turns her face to the side, looking back at me.

"My queen." I run my hands over her skin and she shifts her hips. "You should stop, or I will fuck you again right now."

She sucks in a breath as her hips shift once more.

"Reyna." I grab her chin and force her mouth back to mine, kissing her deep and letting her taste herself on my tongue. "You need to rest. Get back in the tub."

She rises slowly and does as I said but rebels by washing herself as she stands in the water, letting me watch.

Climbing off the bed, I grab the towel we hadn't used before and wrap it around her. Then I go to the chair in the corner and pick up the clothes I got for her. She can wear them tomorrow, because tonight, I want to feel her skin. I just hope I've convinced her not to do as she planned.

She stays wrapped in the towel as she sits on the bed, watching me as I dress.

"I'm going to go get us some food. Stay here." I lean down and kiss her gently, the dark hunger sated.

"Where would I go?" She murmurs when I pull back.

"Where, indeed." I turn and stride out, leaving her to wonder at my response.

She is still there when I return with a tray, only she has pulled on the dark red shirt I had left out. It looks good against her pale skin.

189

"What did you mean?" She asks as I climb on the bed and set the food between us.

"I mean that I saw your face and I know you have a stupid idea in your head."

She swallows but doesn't deny it.

"So what did you do?" Because I know she did something.

"I sent a message." She drops the bomb like nothing. "I'm leaving to keep you all safe."

"Not without me." My tone brooks no argument.

"Hagen, no." She shakes her head.

"Reyna." I just stare at her. "We will leave tonight after full dark. Call in the clouds. Make a storm like you did before."

"I don't know how I did it."

"Try," I urge.

She sits on the bed, her legs crossed, and lets her eyes close. I feel the subtle shift in her, and a light begins to surround her. Magic. The clouds move in and the waters grow wild. She opens her eyes and looks out the window, a smile curving her lips.

"I don't want you to come."

"I'm sorry but I can't let you go alone, my queen," I pledge.

She crawls around the tray and kisses me softly. "I command you not to come."

"I will do anything for you but that. I love you."

"You don't know me," she argues.

"I know you well enough. Do you think you could love me?"

"I think I'm half in love with you already," she answers softly.

"Then it is settled. We will protect them," I tell her.

I leave her on the bed to go tell Travis our plan. She is asleep when I get back, curled on her side. She looks like home. I lie down with her until after midnight. I wake her as I sit up.

Travis has done what I asked and the Black Wolf has fallen back away from my brothers' ships. I help her up and she pulls on the black leather pants that I knew would fit her like a glove.

"I don't like this."

* * *

HE WON'T LISTEN but then, I didn't expect him to and maybe I don't want him to. We sail away from them, and I stand on the deck, calling for the wind to blow, to fill the sails. It blows my hair and the darkness hides my tears.

Hagen is at my back, and I know he can feel my muscles tense.

"They will understand," he purrs against my ear. "Eventually." He kisses my neck and I lean back. "We'll get away and then you can see if you can figure out the way we need to go."

I just hope whatever is buried calls to me as it is calling the evil in the world.

I'm thankful Hagen is with me; his love roars louder than my fears.

THE END

ACKNOWLEDGMENTS

I am forever grateful for my family for their never-ending support. The encouragement from my best friend Jen. The editing and sounding board of Summer.

And for the readers. The ones that take a chance on my stories. The ones that come back because they fall for the characters.

Thank You.

ABOUT THE AUTHOR

S Lawrence is an emerging author of paranormal fantasy. She is a mom, a wife, a veteran and a fangirl. She lives just outside New Orleans and can be often found wandering the streets of the Quarter.

To sign up for her newsletter to keep up to date on new releases and get in on some awesome giveaways head over to her website at https://www.slawrencewriter.com/

To join her reader group the Myth Mavens go to https://www.facebook.com/groups/1946397745641272/